Leon

Catalogue of first editions of American authors

poets, philosophers, historians, statesmen, essayists, dramatists, novelists,

travellers, humorists

Leon

Catalogue of first editions of American authors
*poets, philosophers, historians, statesmen, essayists, dramatists, novelists,
travellers, humorists*

ISBN/EAN: 9783741189814

Manufactured in Europe, USA, Canada, Australia, Japa

Cover: Foto ©Andreas Hilbeck / pixelio.de

Manufactured and distributed by brebook publishing software
(www.brebook.com)

Leon

Catalogue of first editions of American authors

PREFACE.

A hopeful sign of future book-collecting is exhibited in the fact that the Bibliophiles of America are emulating their brethren of the Old World in placing upon their shelves first editions. But the "editiones principes" sought by wise and patriotic collectors are neither Guttenberg's, Caxton's, Aldus' nor Bodoni's. Amateurs are winnowing from the ripe harvest of books early specimens of those authors in whom the nation takes pride.

As the English collector hunts for Shakspeare, Milton, Thackeray or Shelley, the French for Ronsard, Villon, Montaigne, Musset and Hugo, so the prudent American delves into stores and catalogues for copies of Mather, Franklin, Irving, Poe, Prescott, Longfellow, Lowell, Aldrich, and the rest of the guild of our more famous writers.

Blurred in type and printed on indifferent paper, as some of them are, these first examples of the writings of our great authors are to-day, in many cases, worth their weight in gold. Not only are they of increasing value day by day, but they are of the highest bibliographical and literary interest.

In the first editions the text appears fresh from the author's mind—before those changes which are apt to occur, either from reflection or as the result of unfavorable criticism. Moreover, they often contain passages or poems which are omitted from later editions. It will thus be seen that by collecting the first editions of an Author we have the benefit of a pure and unchanged text. Poor and unassuming as some of these editions appear to us now, they have a distinct personality, which is entirely wanting in the most sumptuous modern editions.

The lack of time has prevented our including other names deserving a place in this catalogue, but it is our intention to publish additional lists from time to time. Believing that, in offering this catalogue, the compilers are supplying a want which is generally felt among American collectors, they trust that due indulgence will be made for errors.

LEON & BROTHER.

New York, 1885.

NOTE.—The works are all First American editions, or such revised editions as from important additional matter first published in them, deserve a place in the list. Such revised editions are always invariably noted. The books are perfect, and if not in their original or other well-preserved binding, are encased in cloth or boards. The star prefixed to the name of an Author indicates that the list is believed to comprise all his works published in separate form. Great care has been taken to ascertain the correct date of every 1st edition, in a separate form; but as it is the first attempt to compile such a Catalogue some few mistakes may have occured—caused by the contradictions of Bibliographical Works, the forgetfulness of Authors themselves and the practice of Publishers of post-dating their books. Correction of any error will be thankfully received, and the Book not correctly described may be returned to us at our own expense.

The lack of date shows that it could not be correctly ascertained. Some works may have been illustrated although not so noted.

We beg our customers to send remittance by Draft, Money Order or Registered Letter. We are not responsible for money sent otherwise.

" Gentlemen, hear him : He tells you, and very truly, that he has been indefatigable in his inquiries after an answer to the only question that at all concerns him ; viz.—'Which is the Princeps Editio, and which is not ?' "—BIBLIOSOPHIA.

Adams, Mrs. Abigail.
Letters. Edit. by Ch. Fr. Adams. 2 vols. 12mo. Bost. 1840. $2.00

Adams, Ch. Follen.
Leedle Yawcob Strauss, and other Poems. 12mo. Bost. 1880. 1.00

Adams, John,
Born at Braintree, Mass., 1753, d. 1826.

The Defense of the Constitution of the U. S. 3 vols. 8vo.
    Phila. 1797.. 3.50
Works, with Life of the Author, by Ch. Fr. Adams. 10 vols.
    8vo. Bost. 1850-6 .... 15.00

Adams, J. J.
The Charter Oak. 8vo. N. Y. 1839...................... 1.25

Adams, John Quincy,
Born at Quincy, Mass., 1767 d. 1848.

Poems. 16mo. N. Y. 1848......................... .... 1.25
Memoirs. Edit. by Ch. Fr. Adams. 12 vols. 8vo. Phil. 1874-6 40.00

Alden, Timothy,
Born 1771, d. 1839.

A Collection of American Epitaphs, etc. 5 vols. 16mo.
    N. Y. 1814.. 10.00

*Aldrich, Thomas B.

Born at Portsmouth, New Hamp., 1836,

The Bells. 12mo, N. Y. 1855.......................	3.00
Daisy's Neclace. 12mo, N. Y. 1857...............	2.00
The Course of True Love, etc. 12mo, N. Y. 1858.........	2.00
The Ballad of Babie Bell, etc. 12mo, N. Y. 1859.........	2.25
Pampinea. 12mo, N. Y. 1861.....................	2.50
Out of His Head. 12mo, N. Y. 1862................	2.00
Poems (Portrait.) 32mo, N. Y. 1863..............	3.50
Poems. 32mo, Bost. 1865......................	3.00
Pansy's Wish. Sm. 4to, Bost. (1867).............	2.00
Story of a Bad Boy. Illus. 12mo, Bost. 1870..............	2.50
Marjorie Daw. 12mo, Bost. 1873.........	1.75
Cloth of Gold. 12mo, Bost. 1874................	1.75
Prudence Palfrey. 12mo, Bost. 1875..................	1.75
Flower and Thorn. 12mo, Bost. 1877............	1.25
A Rivermouth Romance. 12mo, Bost. 1877............	1.50
The Queen of Sheba. 12mo, Bost. 1877.	1.50
The Story of a Cat, (transl.) Ill. 12mo, Bost. 1879.....	1.00
The Stillwater Tragedy. 12mo, Bost. 1880.	1.00
Friar Jerome's Beautiful Book (collected.) 12mo, Bost. 1881	1.00
XXXVI Lyrics and XII Sonnets (collected.) 12mo, Bost. 1881	1.00
Poems (Illustrated.) 8vo, Bost. 1882..................	2.50
From Pankopag to Pesth. 12mo, Bost. 1883.	1.25
Mercedes and later Lyrics. 12mo, Bost. 1884............	1.00
Marjorie Daw, (with additions.) 16mo, Bost. 1885.........	1.00

Allen, B. (Osander.)

Miscel. Poems. 12mo, Hudson, 1811	1.50

Allston, Washington,

Born at Georgetown, S. C., 1779, d. 1843.

The Sylphs of the Seasons. 12mo, Bost. 1813..............	2.00

Ashe, S. M.

La Gran Quivera. 12mo, N. Y. 1852.....................	1.25

Bailey, James M.

Life in Danbury. 12mo, Boston, 1873....................	1.00

Baker, W. S.

American Engravers and their Works. 12mo, Phila. 1875...	1.25

*Bancroft, George,

Born in Worcester, Mass., 1800.

Poems. 8vo, Cambr. 1823.	15.00
Politics of Ancient Greece (transl. from Heeren.) 8vo, Boston, 1824...........	3.00

Oration at Northampton. 8vo, North. 1826................ 3.00
Hist. of Political System of Europe (transl. from Heeren) 2 vols.
    8vo, North. 1829................................... 5.00
►History of the United States. 8vo, Bost., vol. I, 1834; vol. II.
    1837; vol. III, 1840; vol. IV, 1852; vol. V, 1853;
    vol. VI, 1854; vol. VII, 1858; vol. VIII, 1860; vol. IX,
    1866; vol. X, 1875................................... 75.00
Oration Delivered at Springfield. 8vo, Springfield, 1836.... 3.00
History of Colonization of United States (abridged). 2 vols.
    12mo, Boston, 1841................................ 3.50
Oration on Death of Jackson. 8vo, 1845 .... 2.50
Oration on Progress, etc., of Human Race. 8vo, N. Y., 1854 2.00
Miscellanies. 8vo, N. Y., 1855 .... 3.00
Memorial Address on Lincoln (Port.) 8vo, Washington, 1866 . 1.00
History of the Formation of the Constitution of the United
    States. 2 vols. 8vo, N. Y. 1882.................... 4.00
History of the United States (re-written and revised). 6 vols.
    8vo, N. Y., 1884-5................................ 12.00

Bancroft, Hubert Howe.
Born in Ohio, 1832.

The Native Races of Pacific Coast. 5 vols. 8vo, San Fran. 1882. 22.50

Barker, James N.
Born at Phila., Penn.

Tears and Smiles. 18mo, Phila. 1808..................... 2.00
The Indian Princess. 18mo, N. Y. 1808.................. 1.75
Marmion. 18mo, N. Y. 1816............................. 1.50
How to Try a Lover. 18mo, N. Y. 1817................. 1.50

*Barlow, Joel,
Born at Reading, Conn. 1755, d. 1812.

The Prospect of Peace. New Haven, 1778 .... 7.50
Elegy on T. Hosmer. 8vo, Hartford, 1780.............. 5.00
The Vision of Columbus. 12mo, Hartford, 1787 .... 3.50
The Conspiracy of Kings. 8vo, Newburyport, 1794. .... 4.50
The Hasty Pudding. 8vo, New Haven, 1796 .... 5.00
The Columbiad. (Ills.) 4to, Philadelphia, 1807 .... 12.50

Barrett, S. A.,
Mont. 12mo, New York, 1849 .... 1.25

Bartlett, John Russell,
Born in Rhode Island 1805.

Dictionary of Americanisms. 8vo, New York, 1848 .... 1.50
Personal Narrative of Explorations in Texas, New Mexico, Cali-
    fornia, etc. 2 vol. 8vo, New York, 1854 .... 6.00
Dictionary of Americanisms. Improv. and rev. ed. 8vo, Bos-
    ton, 1859 .... 2.25

Beach, L.
Jonathan Postfree. 18mo, New York, 1807................ 1.00

Beecher, Henry W.
Born at Litchfield, Conn., 1813.

Lectures to Young Men. 16mo, Boston, 1846 .... 3.00
Star Papers. 12mo, New York, 1855 .... 1.25
Life Thoughts. 12mo, Boston, 1858 .... 1.25
Eyes and Ears. 12mo, Boston, 1862 .... 1.25
Address in Manchester. 8vo, New York, 1863. .... 1.50
Freedom and War. 12mo, Boston, 1863. .... 1.50

Belknap, Jeremy.
Born in Massachusetts 1744, d. 1798.

History of New Hampshire, vol. 1 Philadelphia 1784, vol. 2
   Boston 1791, vol. 3 Boston 1792. 3 vols. 8vo. 6.00

Benjamin, S. G.
Constantinople, Isle of Pearls, etc. 12mo, Boston, 1860 ...... 1.00

Benjamin, Park.
Born at Demerara, Guiana 1809, d. 1864.

Poetry. A Satire. 8vo, New York, 1842 .... 1.00

Bliss, P.
Hold the Fort. (Ills) sm. 4to, Boston, 1877 .... 1.00

*Boker, George H.
Born at Philadelphia 1824.

Calaynos a Tragedy. 12mo, Philadelphia, 1848 .... 2.00
Anne Boleyn, a Tragedy. 12mo, Philadelphia, 1850 .... 1.25
The Podesta Daughter and other Poems. 12mo, Philadelphia,
   1852 .... 1.25
Plays and Poems (collected). 2 vols. 16mo, Boston, 1856 ... 2.50
Poems of the War. 12mo, Boston, 1864 .... 1.75
Konigsmark and other Poems. 12mo, Philadelphia, 1869 .... 1.00
The Book of the Dead. 12mo, Philadelphia, 1882........... 1.25

Bolles, J. R.
Solitude and Society. 12mo, New York, 1846 .... 1.00

Booth, Mrs. M.
Wayside Blossoms. 16mo, Philadelphia, 1865 .... 1.00

Bradstreet, Mrs. Anna.
Born 1613, d. 1672.

Several Poems etc. 2d ed. (1st Amer.) enlarged. Bost., 1678. 20.00
The Works—Prose and Verse (edited by Ellis). 8vo, Charleston, 1867 .... 12.00

Brainard, John G. C.
Born at New London, Conn., 1796, d. 1828.

Occasional Pieces of Poetry. 8vo, New York, 1825. ....   3.00

Brainerd, Erastus.
Millais, J. E. (Ills.) 4to, Boston, 1878. ....   4.00

Branagan, T.
Avenia, a tragical Poem. 12mo, Philadelphia, 1805 ....   2.00

Brooks, Charles T.
Born at Salem, Mass., 1813, d. 1883.

A Poem. 8vo, Boston, 1845 ....   2.00
Aquidneck. 16mo, Providence, 1848 ....   1.50
German Lyrics. 12mo, Boston, 1853 ....   1.25
Faust [transl.] 12mo, Boston, 1856 ....   1.25
The Jobsiad. 12mo, Philadelphia, 1863 ....   1.00

Brougham, J.
Life in New York. 12mo, New York, 1856................   1.00
Columbus El Filibustero. 12mo, New York, 1857 ....   1.25
Take care of little Charley. 12mo, New York, 1858 ....   1.00

Brown, Charles Brockden.
Born at Philadelphia 1771, d. 1810.

Alcuin, a dialogue on the Rights of Women. 1797 ....   4.00
Wieland. 1798 ....   7.50
Ormond. New York, 1799 ....   6.00
Arthur Mervyn. 1st part. Philadelphia, 1799..............   3.75
       "   2nd part. 1800 ....   3.50
Edgar Huntley. 1801 ....   4.00
Clara Howard. 1801 ....   4.25
Jane Talbot. 1804......................................   3.50

Brown, J. W.
Michael Agonistes. 12mo, New York, 1843 ....   1.50

Brown, S.
Essay on American Poetry, etc. 12mo, New Haven, 1818....   2.50

Browne, Ch. F. (Artemus Ward.)
Born at Waterford, Maine, 1834, d. 1867.

Artemus Ward. His Travels Among the Mormons. 12mo, New   30.00
       York, 1866...............................   1.25
       "   in London· 12mo, New York, 1867..........   1.00

*Bryant, William Cullen.
Born at Cummington, Mass. 1794, d. 1878.

The Embargo. 1808 ....   3.00
       "   2d ed. enlarged. 12mo, Boston, 1809 ....   15.00
Poems. 12mo, Cambridge, 1821 ....   10.00

Misc. Poems selected from United States Literary Gazette (with
    some original Poems by W. C. B.) 12mo, Boston, 1826. 15.00
Poems, 12mo, New York, 1832 .... 6.50
Poems. 12mo, New York, 1836 .... 3.00
Selections from Am. Poets (edited). 18mo, New York, 1840.. 2.00
The Fountain. 12mo, New York, 1842...................... 3.00
White Footed Deer. 18mo, New York, 1844 .... 5.00
Poems. 12mo, 1846 .... 2.00
Funeral Oration. 1848 .... 1.50
'Letters of a Traveller. 12mo, New York, 1850.............. 1.50
Poems. 2 vols. 12mo, New York, 1854.................... 2.50
Letters from a Traveller. 2d series. 12mo, New York, 1859 . 1.50
·Discource on W. Irving. sm. 4to, New York, 1860......... 1.00
Forest Hymn (Ills.) 4to, New York, 1860 .... 3.00
Poems. 1863 .... 2.00
·Thirty Poems. 12mo, New York, 1864..................... 2.00
Festival at Century Club. 8vo, New York, 1865 .... 2.00
Letters from the East. 1869 .... 1.25
Discourse on Life of E. Verplanck. 8vo, New York, 1870.... 2.00
Homer's Illiad (transl.) 2 vols, 8vo, Boston, 1870 .... 7.50
Homer's Odyssei (transl.) 2 vols, 8vo, Boston, 1871........ 10.00
Song of the Sower. (Ills.) 4to, 1871 .... 3.00
Picturesque America (edited). 2 vols, 4to, New York, 1872. 25.00
Little People of the Snow. sm. 4to, New York, 1873........ 2.50
Orations and Adresses. 12mo, New York, 1873 .... 1.50
Popular History of United States (with S. H. Gay). 4 vols,
    8vo, New York. 1876 .... 12.50
Poetical Works (edited by P. Godwin). 2 vols, 8vo, New York,
    1883 .... 4.50
Prose Writings ed. by P. Godwin. 2 vols, 8vo, N. Y., 1884... 4.50

Bulkley, C. H. A.

Niagara, A Poem. 12mo, New York, 1848............... 1.25

Burleigh, W. H.

Poems. 12mo, Philadelphia, 1841 .... 1.25

*Burroughs, John.
Born in New York, 1837.

Notes on W. Whitman. 1867 .... 1.75
Wake Robin. 16mo, New York, 1871 .... 2.50
Winter Sunshine. 16mo, New York, 1875 .... 1.75
Birds and Poets. 12mo, Boston, 1877..................... 1.75
·Locust and Wild Honey. 12mo, Boston, 1879 .... 2.00
Pepacton and other sketches. 12mo, Boston, 1881 .... ·1.25
Fresh Fields. 12mo, Boston, 1885 .... 1.25

Butler, W. A.

Nothing to Wear (Ills). 12mo, New York, 1857............ 1.25
·Two Millions (Ills). 12mo, New York, 1858......... 1.25

Cable, George W.
Old Creole Days. 12mo, New York, 1879.................... 1.00

Calhoun, John C.
Born in Abbeville, S. C. 1782, *d.* 1850.
Works, edited by R. K. Cralle. 6 vols, 8vo, New York, 1853-4 12.00

Calvert, G. H.
Poems. 16mo, Boston, 1847........................ .... 2.00
Arnold and Andre. 8vo, Boston, 1864 ... . 2.00

Carey, Henry C.
Born at Philadelphia, Pa. 1793, *d.* 1879.
Principles of Political Economy. 3 vols, 8vo, 1837-40........ 7.50
The Past, the Present and the Future. 8vo, Philadelphia, 1848 2.00
Principles of Social Science. 3 vols, 8vo, Philadelphia, 1858-60 2.50
The Unity of Law. 8vo, Philadelphia, 1873.............. 2.50

Carleton, Will, M.
Farm Ballads. 4to, New York, 1873 .... 1.50

Catlin, George.
Born in Pennsylvania 1796, *d* 1872.
Manners, Customs, etc. of North Amer. Indians (Ills). 2 vols,
    8vo, New York, 1841 .... 8.00

Channing, Will. E.
Born at Newport, R. I. 1780, *d.* 1842.
Slavery. 12mo, Boston, 1835 .... 1.50
Works (collected ed.) 5 vols, 12mo, 1841.................. 5.00

Channing, W. E.
Poems. 16mo, Boston, 1843............................. 1.25
Poems 2d series. 16mo, Boston, 1847....................... 1.00
The Woodman. 16mo, Boston, 1849....................... 1.00

Cheever, Henry T.
The Whale and his Captors (Ills.) 12mo, New York, 1850 .. 1.00
The Island World of the Pacific. 12mo, New York, 1851 .... 1.00
Life in the Sandwich Island. 12mo, New York 1.25

Child, Mrs. Lydia M.
Letters from New York. 12mo, New York, 1843............ 1.25
    "   2d series. 12mo, New York, 1845.... 1.00

Chivers, T. H.
Nacooche with other Poems. 12mo, New York, 1837........ 1.25
The Lost Pleiad. 8vo, New York, 1845.................... 1.00

Claflin, Tennie C.

Constitutional Equality a Right of Woman. Portr. 8vo, New
York, 1871.. 1.00

*Clarke, McDonald.
Born 1798. d. 1842.

The Elixir of Moonshine. 18mo, Gotham, 5822 .... 5.00
The Gossip. 18mo, New York, 1823...................... 4.00
Death in Disguise. 18mo, Boston, 1833 .... 4.00
Poems. 12mo, New York, 1836 .... 3.50

Clarke, Mrs. S. I. Lippincott, [Grace Greenwood.]
Poems. 16mo, Boston, 1851............................ 1.25

Clay, Henry.
Born in Virginia 1777, d. 1852.

The Life, Correspondence and Speeches—edited by Colton.
6 vols, 8vo, New York, 1857 .... 17.50

*Clemens, Samuel L. [Mark Twain.]
Born at Florida, Mo., 1835.

The Celebrated Jumping Frog etc. 12mo, New York, 1867.. 1.25
Innocents Abroad. (Ills.) 8vo, Hartford, 1869............ 3.00
Autobiography and 1st Romance. 8vo, New York, 1871..... 1.00
Roughing it (Ills.) 8vo, Hartford, 1872 .... 2.75
The Gilded Age (with Chas. D. Warner). 8vo, Hartford, 1873 3.00
Adventures of Tom Sawyer. 8vo, New York, 1876......... 2.00
Sketches Old and New. 4to, New York, 1877............. 2.50
A True Story etc. 32mo, Boston, 1877................... 1.00
A Tramp Abroad. 8vo, New York, 1880 ....: 2.50
The Prince and Pauper. 8vo, Boston, 1882 .... 2.50
The Stolen White Elephant. 12mo, 1882........ .. .. 1.00
Life on the Mississippi. 8vo, Boston, 1883 .... 2.75
Adventures of Hucklebery Finn. 4to, 1885 .... 2.75

Colton, Walter.
Born in Vermont 1797, d. 1851.

Deck and Port. Ills. 12mo, New York, 1850............. 1.50
Three Years in California. 12mo, New York, 1850... ...... 1.25
Ship and Shore. 12mo, New York, 1851................. 1.25

Cook, Clarence.
Born in Massachusetts 1828.

The House Beautiful. Ills. New York................... 5.00

Cook, W.
Sunbeam. 18mo, Salem, 1853 .... 1.25
The Fragments. 16mo, Salem, 1862...................... 1.00

Cooke, John E.
Born at Winchester, Va., 1830.

The Virginia Comedians. 12mo, New York 2.00
Henry St. John. 12mo, New York 1.00
Wearing of the Gray. Ills. 8vo, New York, 1867 .... 2.00

* Cooper, James F.
Born at Burlington, N. J., 1789, d. 1851.

Precaution. 2 vols. 12mo, New York, 1820 .... 6.00
The Spy. 2 vols. 12mo, New York, 1821 .... 5.00
The Pioneers. 2 vols. 12mo, New York, 1823 .... 4.00
The Pilot. 2 vols. 12mo, New York, 1823................. 4.00
Lionel Lincoln. 2 vols. 12mo, New York, 1825 .... 3.50
Last of the Mohicans. 2 vols. 12mo, Philadelphia, 1826..... 3.00
The Prairies. 2 vols. 12mo, Philadelphia, 1827 .... 3.00
Red Rover. 2 vols. 12mo, Philadelphia, 1828............ 3.00
Notions of the Americans. 2 vols. 12mo, Philadelphia, 1828.. 3.00
The Wept of Wish-ton-Wish. 2 vols. 12mo, Philadelphia, 1829 3.00
The Water Witch. 2 vols. 12mo, Philadelphia, 1830 .... 2.50
The Bravo. 2 vols. 12mo, Philadelphia, 1831 .... 2.25
The Heidenmauer. 2 vols. 12mo, Philadelphia, 1832........ 2.25
The Headsman. 2 vols. 12mo, Philadelphia, 1833 .... 2.25
A Letter to his Countrymen. 12mo, New York, 1834........ 2.50
Sketches of Switzerland. 4 vols. 12mo, Philadelphia, 1836 .. 5.00
Gleaning in Europe—France. 2 vols. 12mo, Philadelphia, 1837 2.50
" England. 2 vols. 12mo, Philadelphia, 1837 . 2.50
" Italy. 2 vols. 12mo, Philadelphia, 1838.... 2.50
Homeward Bound. 2 vols. 12mo, Philadelphia, 1838........ 1.75
The American Democrat. Cooperstown, 1838............... 1.75
The Chronicles of Cooperstown. Cooperstown, 1838 .... 2.50
Home as Found. 2 vols. 12mo, Philadelphia, 1838 .... 1.25
The History of the Navy of United States. 2 vols. 8vo, Philadelphia, 1839 .... 3.50
The Pathfinder. 2 vols. 12mo, Philadelphia, 1840 .... 2.00
Mercedes of Castile. 2 vols. 12mo, Philadelphia, 1840 .... 1.75
The Deerslayer. 2 vols. 12mo, Philadelphia, 1841 .... 1.75
History of the Navy of United States, abridged. 12mo, Philadelphia, 1841.............................. 1.50
The Two Admirals. 2 vols. 12mo, Philadelphia, 1842........ 1.50
The Wing and Wing. 2 vols. 12mo, Philadelphia, 1842...... 1.50
The Battle of Lake Erie. 12mo, Cooperstown, 1843 .... 1.50
Ned Meyers. 12mo, Philadelphia, 1843............... 1.50
Wyandotte. 2 vols. 12mo, Philadelphia, 1843 .... 1.50
Case of A. G. Mackenzie with Review. 12mo, New York, 1844 1.75
Afloat and Ashore or M. Wallingford. 2 vols. 12mo, Philadelphia, 1844 .... 1.75
Satanstoe. 2 vols. 12mo, New York, 1845................. 1.25
The Chainbearer. 2 vols. 12mo, New York, 1846 .... 1.25
The Red Skins. 2 vols. 12mo, New York, 1846 .... 1.25
Lives of American Naval Officers. 2 vols. 12mo, Phil. 1846.. 2.50

The Crater. 2 vols. 12mo, New York, 1847................ 1.00 ~ 1.50
Jack Tier. 2 vols. 12mo, New York, 1848 .... 1.50
Oak Opening. 2 vols. 12mo, New York, 1848............. 1.25
The Sea Lions. 2 vols. 12mo, New York, 1849 .... 1.50
The Ways of the Hour. 12mo, New York, 1850 .... 1.00 ~ 75
History of the Navy, with additions. 8vo, New York, 1853 .. 1.50

Coxe, Arthur C.
Born in New Jersey 1818.

Christian Ballads. 12mo, New York, 1840................. 2.50

Cozzens, F. S.

Acadia. 12mo, New York, 1859 .... 1.50

Cranch, C. P.
Born in Virginia 1813.

Poems. 16mo, Philadelphia, 1844 .... 1.25
Eneid of Virgil (translated). 8vo, Boston, 1872 .... 3.00

Currie, Mrs. Helen.

Poems. 16mo, Philadelphia, 1818 .... 1.50

Curtis, George Ticknor.
Born at Watertown, Mass., 1812.

History of the Constitution of United States. 2 vols, 8vo, New
    York, 1854-8................................ 8.00
Life of D. Webster. 2 vols, 8vo, New York, 1870 .... 4.00

*Curtis, George W.
Born at Providence, R. I., 1824.

Nile Notes of a Howadji. 12mo, New York, 1851 .... 1.50
The Howadji in Syria. 12mo, New York, 1852 .... 2.00
Lotus Eating. 12mo, New York, 1852 .... 1.75
The Potifar Papers. 12mo, New York, 1853............. 3.00
Prue and I. 12mo, New York, 1857 .... 1.50
Trumps. 12mo, New York, 1861 .... 2.00
An Oration and Rhyme of Rhode Island. 8vo, N. York, 1863 1.50
Bryant, W. C., Life and Writings. 4to, New York, 1879 ... 1.00
Wendel Phillips, Eulogy. 8vo, New York, 1884 ....

Curtis, J. W.

Poems. 12mo, New York, 1846 .... 1.25

*Dana, Richard H.
Born at Cambridge, Mass., 1787, d. 1879.

The Idle Man. 5 Nos. 8vo, New York, 1821 .... 7.50
Poems. 16mo, Boston, 1827............................ 5.00
A Poem delivered at Andover. 8vo, Boston, 1829 .... 3.00
Poems and Prose Writings. 12mo, Philadelphia, 1833 ...... 3.50
       "   (collected). 2 vols. New York, 1850.. 2.50

to E quo a $1.00 gro'd road
Trumps " " 1.50 " " "

Dana R H Jr

The Seaman's Friend plates N Y 1842 2d ed 50c qp

To Cuba & back N Y 1859 qus a 1.00 with autograph of
Frank Vincent - Jr

Speech Reorganization of the Rebel States Boston
1865 Pamphlet - 25c qus a

Dana, R. H. Jr.
Two Years before the Mast. 12mo, New York, 1869 .... 1.50

*Davidson, Lucretia M.
Born at Plattsburg, New York, 1808.
Amir Khan and other Poems. 12mo, New York, 1829 ...... 2.00

Davis, Jefferson.
Born in Kentucky 1808.
The Rise and Fall of the Confederate Gov't. Ills. 2 vols.
    8vo, New York, 1881 .... 6.00

Dawes, R.
The Valley of the Nashaway. 12mo, Boston, 1830 .... 1.50

De Cordova, R.
The Prince's Visit. Ills. 8vo, New York, 1861 .... 1.25

Denslow, V. B.
Manhatta. 16mo, New York, 1856........................ 1.00

Derby, G. H. (John Phœnix.)
Born in Massachusetts 1824, d. 1861.
Phœnixiana—Sketches and Burlesques. 12mo, New York, 1855 1.25
Squibob Papers. 1859 .... 1.00

Dodge, Miss Mary (Gail Hamilton).
Born in Massachusetts 1838.
Country Living and Thinking. 12mo, Boston, 1862.......... 1.25
Womans Wrongs. 12mo, Boston, 1868 .... 1.50
Battle of the Books. 12mo, Boston, 1870 .... 1.25

*Drake, Joseph Rodman.
Born at New York 1795, a. 1820.
Poems by Croaker & Co. (with Halleck). 18mo, New York, 1819 12.50
The Culprit Fay and other Poems. 8vo, New York, 1835.... 3.00
The American Flag. 4to, New York, 1861 .... 1.25

*Dunlap, William.
Born at Perth Amboy, N. J., 1766, d. 1839.
Darby's Return. 8vo, New York, 1787 .... 4.00
The Archers. 8vo, New York, 1796 .... 4.00
Tell Truth and Shame the Devil. 8vo, 1797................ 3.00
Andre, Tragedy. 8vo, New York, 1798.................... 15.00
The Virgin of the Sun. 8vo, New York, 1800 .... 2.00
Pizaro in Peru. 8vo, New York, 1800 .... 1.25
False Shame. 18mo, New York, 1800... .... 1.25
The Wild Goose Chase. 8vo, New York, 1800 .... 1.50
Abaellino. 18mo, New York, 1803........................ 1.25
Ribbemont. 18mo, New York, 1803 .... 1.00

Dana R H Jr
The Seaman's Friend plates NY 1842 2d ed 50c gp?
To Cuba & back N Y 1859 gpo a 1.00 with autograph of
    Frank Vincent Jr
Speech Reorganization of the Rebel States Boston
1865 Pamphlet 25c gpo a

Dana, R. H. Jr.

Two Years before the Mast. 12mo, New York, 1869 .... 1.50

*Davidson, Lucretia M.
Born at Plattsburg, New York, 1808.

Amir Khan and other Poems. 12mo, New York, 1829 ...... 2.00

Davis, Jefferson.
Born in Kentucky 1808.

The Rise and Fall of the Confederate Gov't. Ills. 2 vols.
8vo, New York, 1881 .... 6.00

Dawes, R.

The Valley of the Nashaway. 12mo, Boston, 1830 .... 1.50

De Cordova, R.

The Prince's Visit. Ills. 8vo, New York, 1861 .... 1.25

Denslow, V. B.

Manhatta. 16mo, New York, 1856....................... 1.00

Derby, G. H. (John Phœnix.)
Born in Massachusetts 1824, d. 1861.

Phœnixiana—Sketches and Burlesques. 12mo, New York, 1855 1.25
Squibob Papers. 1859 .... 1.00

Dodge, Miss Mary (Gail Hamilton).
Born in Massachusetts 1838.

Country Living and Thinking. 12mo, Boston, 1862.......... 1.25
Womans Wrongs. 12mo, Boston, 1868 .... 1.50
Battle of the Books. 12mo, Boston, 1870 .... 1.25

*Drake, Joseph Rodman.
Born at New York 1795, d. 1820.

Poems by Croaker & Co. (with Halleck). 18mo, New York, 1819 12.50
The Culprit Fay and other Poems. 8vo, New York, 1835.... 3.00
The American Flag. 4to, New York, 1861 .... 1.25

*Dunlap, William.
Born at Perth Amboy, N. J., 1766, d. 1839.

Darby's Return. 8vo, New York, 1787 .... 4.00
The Archers. 8vo, New York, 1796 .... 4.00
Tell Truth and Shame the Devil. 8vo, 1797............... 3.00
Andre, Tragedy. 8vo, New York, 1798.................... 15.00
The Virgin of the Sun. 8vo, New York, 1800 .... 2.00
Pizaro in Peru. 8vo, New York, 1800 .... 1.25
False Shame. 18mo, New York, 1800.... .... 1.25
The Wild Goose Chase. 8vo, New York, 1800 .... 1.50
Abaellino. 18mo, New York, 1803....................... 1.25
Ribbemont. 18mo, New York, 1803 .... 1.00

The Voice of Nature. 18mo, New York, 1803 .... 1.25
Wife of Two Husbands. 18mo, New York, 1817............ 1.00
Leicester. 18mo, New York, 1807 .... 1.00
Fontainville Abbey. 18mo, New York, 1807 .... 1.00
Father of an Only Child. 18mo, New York, 1807 .... 1.50
Blunt Boy. 18mo, New York, 1808............ .... 1.25
Fraternal Discord. 18mo, New York, 1809 .... 1.00
Rinaldo Rinaldini. 18mo, New York, 1810 .... 1.00
The Italian Father. 18mo, New York, 1810 .... 1.00
Yankee Chronology. 18mo, New York, 1812 .... 2.00
Memoir of G. F. Cooke. Portr. 2 vols, 16mo, New York, 1813 3.00
A Record of 5 Months in 1813. New York, 1813............ 2.50
Peter the Great. 18mo, New York, 1814 .... 1.00
The Good Neighbour. 18mo, New York, 1814............ .. 1.00
Lovers' Vow. 18mo, New York, 1814 .... 1.00
Life of Ch. B. Brown. 2 vols, 12mo, Philadelphia, 1815 .... 3.50
The Glory of Columbus. 18mo, New York, 1817 .... 1.50
A Trip to Niagara. 18mo, New York, 1830 .... 1.25
History of American Theatre. 8vo, New York, 1832 .... 2.50
History of Art of Design in the United States. 2 vols. 8vo,
    New York, 1834 .... 20.00
30 Years Ago. 2 vols. 12mo, New York, 1836 .... 2.50
History of New York for Schools. 2 vols, 16mo, New York 1837 2.00
History of New Netherland and State of New York. 2 vols.
    8vo, New York, 1839 .... 5.00

Duyckinck, Evert A.
Born at New York 1816, d. 1878.

Cyclopedia of American Literature (with G. L. Duyckinck).
    Ills. 2 vols, 8vo, New York, 1855 .... 6.00

Dwight, Timothy.
Born at Northampton, Mass., 1752, d. 1817.

The Conquest of Canaan. 8vo, Hartford, 1785.............. 4.00
Greenfield Hill. 8vo, New York, 1794 .... 2.50
Travels in New England and New York. 4 vols, 8vo, New
    Haven, 1821-2 .... 5.00

Edwards, Jonathan.
Born in Connecticut 1703, d. 1757.

A Careful and Strict Inquiry into the Modern Prevailing No-
    tions of the Freedom of Will. 8vo, Boston, 1754...... 15.00

Eggleston, Edward.

The Hoosier Schoolmaster. 12mo, New York, 1871 .... 1.50
The End of the World. 12mo, New York, 1872 .... 1.50
The Mystery of Metropolisville. 12mo, New York, 1873 .... 1.25
The Circuit Rider. 12mo, New York, 1874 .... 1.25
Roxy. 12mo, New York, 1878 .... 1.25

See Emerson in Falconer 259

*Emerson, Ralph Waldo.
Born at Boston 1803, d. 1882.

Historical Discourse. 1835	7.50
Nature. 12mo, Boston, 1836	12.00
Carlyle Sartos Resartus (edited). 12mo, Boston, 1836	2.00
The American Scholar-Oration. Cambridge, 1837	4.00
Carlyle Miscellanies (edited). 2 vols, 12mo, Boston, 1838	2.50
Address in the Divinity College. 8vo, Cambridge, 1838	4.50
Oration before the Dart. College. 8vo, 1838...............	4.00
The Dial (edited). 4 vols. 4to, Boston, 1841-4	30.00
Man the Reformer. 1841	4.00
Lecture on the Times. 1841.........	3.50
Oration. Method of Nature. 8vo, Boston, 1841	3.50
The Conservative. 1841	3.50
Essays. 12mo. Boston, 1841..............................	6.00
The Transcendentalist. 1842	5.00
Carlyle, Past and Present (edited) 12mo, Boston, 1843	2.00
Essays. 2d Series. 12mo, Boston, 1844	5.00
The Young American. 1844......	3.50
On Emancipation in W. India. 8vo, Boston, 1844	3.50
Poems. 12mo, Boston, 1847.	7.50
Nature, Adresses and Lectures (collected). 12mo, Boston, 1849	3.50
Representative Men. 12mo, Boston, 1850	3.50
Memoir of M. Fuller Ossolli (edited). 2 vols, 12mo, Boston 1852	3.00
Miscellanies. 12mo, Boston 1856..........................	2.00
English Traits. 12mo, Boston, 1856	1.75
Conduct of Life. 12mo, Boston, 1860....................	3.50
The Gullistan by Sadi (edited). 12mo, Boston, 1865	2.00
Poems. Portr. 32mo, Boston, 1865	2.00
Thoreau Letters (edited). 12mo, Boston, 1865..............	2.50
May Day. 12mo, Boston, 1867	2.00
Society and Solitude. 12mo, Boston, 1870..................	1.50
Parnassus (edited). 8vo, Boston, 1874	2.50
Letters and Social Aims. 12mo, Boston, 1876	1.50
Poems (revised). 18mo, Boston, 1878...................	1.50
Fortune of the Republic. 12mo, Boston, 1878	1.00
Miscellanies (collected). 12mo, Boston, 1884	1.50
Lectures and Biographical Studies (collected). 12mo, Boston, 1884	1.25
Poems (collected). 1884	1.25

Emmons, R.
The Fredoniad. 4 vols, 8vo, Boston, 1827	6.00	.80 Bangs.

English, Th. D.
Zephania Doolittle. 12mo, Philadelphia, 1838..............	1.50

Evans, Nathaniel.
Born at Philadelphia 1742, d. 1767.

Poems. 8vo, Philadephia, 1772	10.00

Everest, C. W.

Babylon. 8vo, Hartford, 1838................................ .... 2.00
The Poets of Connecticut (edited). 8vo, Hartford, 1843...... 2.50

Everett, Alexander H.
Born at Boston 1792, d. 1847.

America—General Survey of polit. situation, etc. 8vo, Phila-
 delphia, 1827 .... 2.50
Critical and Misc. Essays. 12mo, 1845 .... 2.50
Poems. 12mo, Boston, 1845................................ 2.50
Critical and Misc. Essays. 2d Series. 1847 .... 1.50

Everett. Edward.
Born at Dorchester, Mass., 1794.

Orations and Speeches. 8vo, Boston, 1836 .... 2.50
 "   3 vols, 8vo, Boston, 1853-8 .... 5.00

Fairfield, S. L.
Born in Massachusetts 1803.

Poems. 18mo, New York, 1823 .... 1.75

Fay, T. S.
Born 1807.

Ulric. 12mo, New York, 1851............................ 1.25

Felton, J. B.

The Horse Shoe: a Poem. 12mo, Cambridge, 1849.......... 1.50

Fessenden, T. G.

Original Poems. 12mo, Philadelphia, 1806 .... 3.00
The Ladies' Monitor. 12mo, B. Falls, 1818................ 2.00

*Fields, J. T.
Born at Portsmouth, N. Hamp., 1820, d. 1881.

Anniversary Poem. 8vo, Boston, 1838 .... 2.00
Poems. Sm. 4to, Boston, 1849 .... 2.25
Poems. 16mo, Cambridge, 1854........................... 2.00
A Few Verses for Few Friends (privately printed). 1858 .... 1.75
Yesterday with Authors. 12mo, Boston, 1872 .... 1.50
Hawthorne. 32mo, Boston, 1876 .... 1.00
Barry Cornwall, etc. 32mo, Boston, 1876................. 1.00
In and Out with Dickens. 32mo, Boston, 1876 .... 1.00
Ballads and other Verses. 1881 .... 1.00

Fiske, John.
Born in Connecticut 1842.

Myths and Myth-Makers. 12mo, Boston, 1872............. 1.50
Outlines of Cosmic Philosophy. 2 vols. 12mo, Boston, 1875 .. 3.50
The Unseen World, etc. 12mo, Boston, 1876............... 1.50

Fay Ts Norman Leslie N.Y 1895 — 2 ung a 75c
    quo a
"   " Ulvie 75c quo a

Franklin's Experiments in Elec at Phil
1760 but at Burgo 21 Jan 86 by
Loron at #175

Excursion of an Evolutionist. 12mo, Boston, 1883 .... 1.50
American Political Ideas. 12mo, New York, 1885 .... 1.00

Francis, J. W.
Born at New York 1789, d. 1861.

Old New York. New York, 1857 .... 2.00
   "   (revised ed.) 12mo, New York, 1858 .... 1.50

Franklin, Benjamin.
Born at Boston, Mass., 1706, d. 1790.

Poor Richard—An Almanack for 1734 (by Rich. Saunders).
    12mo, (Philadelphia,) 1734 .... 50.00
Account of New Invented Fire-Places. 8vo, Philadelphia, 1744 20.00
Interest of Great Britain to her Colonies. 8vo, Boston, 1760.. 15.00
La Science du Bonhomme Richard. 12mo, Philadelphia, 1778 7.50
Way to Wealth. 12mo, Worcester, 1790 .... 6.00
The Life, written by himself. 12mo, Salem, 1796 .... 6.00
Life and Essays (Engr. Title and Portr.) 12mo, New York, pr.
    for H. Gaine 5.00
Works (collected). 6 vols, 8vo, Philadelphia, 1809-17 ...... 9.00
Familiar Letters (ed. by Sparks). 12mo, Boston, 1833 ...... 2.50
Works (ed. by Sparks). 10 vols, 8vo, Boston, 1836-40 ...... 15.00
Works (revised and enlarged). 10 vols. 8vo, Boston, 1858 .... 17.50

*Freneau, Philip.
Born at New York 1752, d. 1832.

A Poem on the Glory of America (with Brackenridge). 12mo,
   Philadelphia, 1772 .... 10.00
The British Prison Ship. 12mo, Philadelphia, 1781 .... 12.00
Poems written chiefly during the late War. 12mo, Philadel-
   phia, 1786 .... 10.00
Miscellaneous Works and Poems. 12mo, Philadelphia, 1788.. 5.00
The Village Merchant. 12mo, Philadelphia, 1794 .... 5.00
Poems written between 1768-94. 12mo, Monmouth, 1795.... 8.50
Poems (revised ed.) 2 vols. 16mo, Philadelphia, 1809........ 4.50
A Laughable Poem, etc. 12mo, Philadelphia, 1809.......... 3.50
A Collection, etc. 2 vols, 12mo, New York, 1815............ 3.50 - .30 Brings

*Fuller-Ossoli, Margaret S.
Born at Cambridge, Mass., 1810, d. 1850.

Eckermann's Conversation with Goethe (translation). 12mo,
   Boston, 1839...... .... 2.00
The Letters of Günderode and Bettine. 1841 .... 2.50
Summer on the Lakes. 12mo, Boston, 1844... .... 4.00
Woman in the 19th Century. 12mo, New York, 1845 ...... 3.00
Papers on Literature and Art. 12mo, New York, 1846 ...... 2.50
At Home and Abroad (Collected by A. B. Fuller). 12mo, Bos-
   ton, 1856 ... . 1.50

Garden, A.

Anecdotes of Revolutionary War (collected). 8vo, Charleston,
1822 .... 3.50
Anecdotes of Revolutionary War (collected). 2d series. 8vo,
Charleston, 1828 .... 3.00

Garrison, W. L.
Born in Massachusetts 1804, d. 1879.

Thought on African Colonization. Boston, 1832 .... 1.50
Sonnets and Poems. 16mo, Boston, 1843 .... 1.50

Gerard, J. W.

Ostrea. 12mo, New York, 1857 .... 1.25

Gilder, Richard W.
Born in New Jersey 1844.

The New Day. 12mo, New York, 1876 .... 1.00
The Poet and his Master (Ills.) 12mo, New York, 1878 .... 1.25

Godfrey, T.
Born in Pennsylvania 1736, d. 1763.

The Court of Fancy. 4to, Philadelphia, 1762 .... 15.00
Juvenile Poems. 4to, Philadelphia, 1765 .... 12.50

Godwin, Parke.

Political Essays. 12mo, 1856 .... 2.00

Grayson, W. J.

Hireling and the Slave. 8vo, Charleston, 1856.............. 1.25

*Greeley, Horace.
Born at Amherst, N. H., 1811, d. 1872.

Protection and Free Trade. 1844 .... 2.00
The Tariff as it is' etc. 12mo, New York, 1844............ 1.50
Association, discussed by Gr. and Raymond. 8vo, 1847 .... 1.50
Hints towards Reforms. 12mo, New York, 1850............ 2.25
Glances at Europe, etc. 12mo, 1851 .... 1.50
The Tariff Question Considered. 1852 .... 1.25
Fuller Ossoli Literature and Art (edited). 12mo, New York,
1852 .... 1.25
Why I am a Whig. 12mo, New York, 1852............... 1.50
Sargent's Life of H. Clay (edited). 12mo, New York, 1852 .. 1.25
What the Arts Teach as to Farming. New York, 1853 ...... 1.00
Love, Marriage and Divorce; Discussion between Gr., James
and Andrews. 1853 .... 1.50
Art and Industry in Crystal Palace (edited). 1853 .... 1.75
Woman in 19th Century by Fuller-Ossoli (edited). 1855 .... 1.50
Controversy between Tribune and G. Smith. New York, 1855 1.50
A History of the Struggle for Slavery Extension. 8vo, New
York, 1856.. 1.75

YA 50c q110 a

A Political Text Book for 1860 (with Cleveland). New York,
1860 .... 1.25
An Overland Journey. New York, 1860 .... 1.50
Divorce: a Correspondence with Owen. New York, 1860 ... 1.50
The American Conflict (Ills.) 2 vols. 8vo Hartford, 1864.6 .. 5.00
Success in Business. New York, 1867 .... 1.25
Letter to Members of Union League Club (privately printed).
1867 .... 2.00
Recollection of a Busy Life. 8vo, New York, 1868 .... 3.00
Essays on Political Economy, etc. 12mo, Boston, 1870 ...... 1.25
What I Know of Farming. 12mo, New York, 1871 ... . 1.25
Letters from Texas and Mississippi. New York, 1871 ...... 1.25
Letter to a Politician (S. Tilden). 8vo, Brooklyn, 1877...... 1.25

Green, A. G.
Old Grimes. 4to, Providence, 1867.......................... 2.00

Griswold, Rufus W.
Born in Vermont, 1815, d. 1857.

The Poets and Poetry of America. 8vo, Philadelphia, 1842 . 1.50
The Female Poets of America. 8vo, Philadelphia, 1860...... 1.50

*Gould, Jay.
History of Delaware Co., N. Y. (Portr.) 12mo, Roxb., 1856. 15.00

Hale, E. E. [Col. F. Ingham].
Born in Boston, Mass., 1822.

Ten Times One is Ten. 12mo, Boston, 1870................ 1.25
A Man without a Country. 16mo, Boston, 1880 .... 1.25

Hall, Mrs. E. B.
Miriam: a Poem. 12mo, Boston, 1837...................... 1.25

*Halleck, Fitz-Greene.
Born at Guilford, Conn., 1795, d. 1867.

Poems by Croaker & Co. (with Drake). 18mo, New York, 1819 12.50
Fanny. 8vo, New York, 1819 .... 7.50
" (with additions). 8vo, New York, 1821 .... 4.00
Alnwick Castle and other Poems. 8vo, New York, 1827 .... 5.00
" (enlarged ed.). 8vo, New York, 1836 .... 2.50
Poems (collected and enlarged ed.) 8vo, New York, 1847.... 3.00
" (enlarged ed.) New York, 1852 .... 2.75
Young America. 12mo, New York, 1865 .... 1.00
Fanny (with add. notes) privately printed. 4to, 1866........ 7.50

*Hamilton, Alexander.
Born in West India 1757, d. 1804.

A Full Vindication of the Measures of Congress. 8vo, New
York, 1774 .... 20.00
Federalist (with Jay and Madison). 2 vols. 16mo, New York,
1788 .... 30.00

Answer to Certain Documents. 8vo, New York, 1800 ...... 9.00
Works. 3 vols. 8vo, New York, 1810...................... 9.00
Official and other Papers, vol. I, (all publ.) 8vo, New York,
    1842 .... 7.50
Works (edited by J. Hamilton). 7 vols, 8vo, New York, 1851. 50.00
History of the Republic (as traced from his writings by J. C.
    Hamilton). 7 vols. 8vo, New York, 1857 .... 25.00

Hamilton, John C.

Life of A. Hamilton (Portr.) 2 vols. 8vo, New York, 1834-40. 10.00

Hammond, W.

Lal. 12mo, New York, 1884.................................. 1.25

Harris, Joel Ch.

Uncle Remus, his Songs and Sayings. 12mo, New York, 1881 1.25

Harte, F. Bret.
Born at Albany, N. Y., 1837.

The Heathen Chinee. 8vo, Chicago, 1870.................. 3.00
East and West Poems. 12mo, Boston, 1871 .... 1.50
Condensed Novels. 12mo, Boston, 1871 .... 1.25
Two Men of Sandy Bar. 18mo, Boston, 1877 .... 1.50
Story of a Mine. 12mo, Boston, 1877...................... 1.00
The Twins of Table Mountain. 16mo, Boston, 1879 .... 1.00
Flip. 18mo, Boston, 1882................................ 1.00
On the Frontier. 12mo, Boston, 1884 .... 1.00

Haslett, A.

Original Poems. 12mo, Boston, 1812...................... 2.00

Hawthorne, Julian.
Born in Massachusetts 1846.

Idolatry. 12mo, Boston, 1874 .... 1.50
Saxon Studies. 12mo, Boston, 1876.... .... 1.50
Dust. 12mo, New York, 1883.............................. 1.25
Beatrix Randolph. 12mo, Boston, 1884 .... 1.25
Nathaniel Hawthorne and his Wife. 2 vols. 12mo, Bost. 1884 3.50

*Hawthorne, Nathaniel.
Born at Salem, Mass., 1804, d. 1864.

Fanshawe, a Tale. 12mo, Boston, 1828.....................
Twice Told Tales. 12mo, Boston, 1837...................... 12.50
Peter Parley Universal History. 2 vols. 12mo, 1837 .... 20.00
The Gentle Boy :a Thrice Told Tale [Plate]. Folio, Boston,
    1839 .... 30.00
Grandfather's Chair. 32mo, Boston, 1841.................. 12.50
Famous Old People. 18mo, Boston, 1841 .... 15.00
Liberty Tree. 18mo, Boston, 1841 .... 15.00
Biographical Stories for Children. 18mo, Boston, 1842 ...... 15.00
Grandfather Chair [revised ed.] 18mo, Boston, 1842........ 7.50

ε α W ρ 1 ευ quo a

Fanaliane 1876 1.25 quo a

Twice Told Tales [enlarged ed.] 2 vols. 16mo, Boston, 1842 . 12.50
A Visit to the Celestial City. 18mo, Philadelphia, [1844].... 6.00
Journal of an African Cruiser [edited]. 12mo, New York, 1845 6.00
Mosses from an Old Manse. 2 parts, 12mo, New York, 1846 . 6.50
The Scarlet Letter. 12mo, Boston, 1850 .... 12.50
    "   2d ed. with a Preface. 12mo, Boston, 1850.... 3.50
True Stories. Ills. 16mo, Boston, 1851 .... 6.00
House of Seven Gables. 12mo, Boston, 1851 .... 4.00
Twice Told Tales [new ed. and pref.] 2 vols, 12mo, Boston,
    1851 .... 4.00
Life of F. Pierce. Portr. 16mo, Boston, 1852 .... 1.50
A Wonder Book. Ills. 18mo, Boston, 1852 .... 7.50
The Snow Image. 12mo, Boston, 1852 .... 3.50
The Blithdale Romance. 12mo, Boston, 1852 .... 2.00
Tanglewood Tales. Ills. 16mo, Boston, 1853 .... 7.50
Mosses from an Old Manse [with additions]. 2 vols, 12mo,
    Boston, 1854 .... 3.50
Marble Faun. 2 vols. 12mo, Boston, 1860 .... 3.00
    "   with addition. 2 vols. 12mo, Boston, 1860........ 3.00
Our Old Home. 12mo, Boston, 1863 .... 3.00
Passages from the American Note Book. 2 vols. 12mo, Boston,
    1868 .... 2.50
    "   "   English Note Book. 2 vols, 12mo, Boston,
    1870 .... 5.00
    "   "   French and Italian Note Book. 2 vols.
    12mo, Boston, 1872....................... 4.00
Septimus Felton. 12mo, Boston, 1872 .... 1.75
The Doliver Romance. 12mo, Boston, 1876................ 1.75
Fanshawe (1st reprint from 1828 ed. with additions). 12mo,
    Boston, 1876................................... 2.00
Dr. Grimshaw's Secret. 12mo, Boston, 1883 .... 1.50
Sketches and Studies. 12mo, Boston, 1883 .... 1.25

Hay, J.

Jim Bludso. 12mo, Boston, 1871.......................... 1.00
Little Breeches. 16mo, Boston, 1871 .... 1.00
Pike County Ballads. 16mo, Boston, 1871... .... 2.50

Hayne, Paul H.

Born at Charleston, S. C., 1831.

Poems. 12mo, Boston, 1855 .... 1.50
Legends and Lyrics. 12mo, Philadelphia, 1872 .... 1.00

Headley, J. T.

The Second War with England. Ills. 2 vols. 12mo, New York,
    1853 .... 3.00
The Chaplains and Clergy of Revolution. 12mo. New York,
    1864 .... 1.50

Higginson, Thomas W.
Born in Massachusetts 1823.

Thalatha (with S. Longfellow). 12mo, Boston, 1853 .. ..   3.00
Woman and Her Wishes. 8vo, Boston, 1853..   ....   2.00
Out-Door Papers. 12mo, Boston, 1869 ....   2.00
Malbone. 16mo, Boston, 1869 ....   1.35
Army Life in a Black Regiment. 12mo, Boston, 1870 ......   1.25
Oldport Days. 1873 ....   1.25
Short Studies of American Authors. 16mo, Boston, 1880 ....   1.00
M. Fuller-Ossoli. Portr. 12mo, Boston, 1884 ....   1.75

Hildreth, R.
Born at Deerfield, Mass., 1807, d. 1865.

Archy Moore. 1837 . ...   2.00
Despotism in America. 12mo, Boston, 1840 ....   1.50
Theory of Morals. 12mo, Boston, 1844 ... .   1.50
History of United States. 6 vols. 8vo, New York, 1849 ......   9.00
Atrocious Judges. 12mo, New York, 1856 ....   1.00

Hilhouse, J. A.

The Judgement. 8vo, New York, 1821 ....   1.50
Hadad: a dramatic Poem. 8vo, New York, 1825 ... .   1.50

Hitchcock, D.

Poetical Works. 12mo, Boston, 1805. ....   2.50
The Social Monitor. 12mo, Stockbridge, 1812. ....   2.00

Hoffman, Chas. F.
Born at New York, 1806.

Winter in the West. 2 vols. 12mo, New York, 1835 ....   2.50
The Vigil of Faith. 12mo, New York, 1842 ....   2.50
The Echo. 8vo, Philadelphia, 1844 ....   2.50
Love's Callendar. 18mo, New York, 1847 ....   1.50

Holland, J. G.
Born at Belchertown, Mass., 1819, d. 1881.

History of Western Massachusetts. 2 vols. 12mo, Springfield,
   1855 ....   3.50
Bitter Sweet. 1858. ....   3.00
Timothy Titcomb's Letters. 12mo, New York, 1858 ....   2.50
Katbrina. New York, 1867 ....   2.00
The Marble Prophecy etc. 12mo, New York, 1872. ....   2.00

*Holmes, Oliver W.
Born at Cambridge, Mass., 1809.

The Harbinger (with P. Benjamin & Sargent). 8vo, Boston,
   1833 ....   10.00
Poems. 12mo, Boston, 1836. ....   8.00
Boylston Prize Dissertation. Boston, 1838 ....   3.50
Homeopathy and its Kindred Delusions. 12mo, Boston, 1842   2.50

JVof F 1 50 quo a

Poems see Next page

Poems 1849 in fair condition 75c quo A

Border line of Knowledge quo a Soiled 50c
8 from the A 1st quotation a Fair cond

Iron Gate New 1st quo a

The Position of Med. Student. Boston, 1844................ 1.75
Urania. 8vo, Boston, 1846 .... 5.00
Lecture in Howard University. 1847...................... 2.00
Poems (enlarged ed.) Portr. 12mo, Boston, 1849 .... 1.50
Poems (enlarged with additions). 12mo, Boston, 1849 ...... 1.50
A Poem, delivered Sept. 9th, 1850. (1850) 1.00
Astrea. 12mo, Boston, 1850............................. 1.00
The Autocrat at the Breakfast Table. Ills. 12mo, Boston, 1858 2.00
Professor at the Breakfast Table. 12mo, Boston, 1860........ 4.00
Currents and Counter Currents. 12mo, Boston, 1861 .... 2.00
Elsie Venner. 2 vols. 12mo, Boston, 1861 .... 3.50
Vive la France, with Everett's Adress. Priv. pr. Camb. (1861) 3.00
Border Line of Knowledge. 12mo, Boston, 1862.. .... 2.00
Songs in Many Keys. 12mo, Boston, 1862 .... 2.00
Oration at Boston. 1863 .... 1.50
Soundings from the Atlantic. 12mo, Boston, 1864 .... 1.50
Humorous Poems. Ills. 18mo, Boston, 1865 .... 1.00
The Guardian Angel. 12mo, Boston, 1867 .... 1.75
Atlantic Almanac (edited with Mitchel). 1868 .... 1.50
Mechanism in Thought and Morals. 12mo, Boston, 1871 .... 2.50
The Claims of Dentistry. 8vo, Boston, 1872............... 1.00
The Poet at Breakfast Table. (Front.) 12mo, Boston, 1872 . 3.50
Songs of many Seasons. 12mo, Boston, 1874 .... 1.50
Poems (new ed. Ills.) 8vo, Boston, 1878 .... 3.00
The School Boy. Ills. 4to, Boston, 1879 .... 2.00
John L. Motley: a Memoir. Portr. 12mo, Boston, 1879...... 2.00
The Iron Gate, etc. Portr. 12mo, Boston, 1880............ 1.50
Pages from an Old Volume of Life (collected). 12mo. Boston,
    1883 .... 1.50
Medical Essays. 12mo, Boston, 1883....''''............. 1.25
The Autocrat at Breakfast Table (revised). 12mo, Boston,
    1883 .... 1.50
The Poet at Breakfast Table (revised). 12mo, Boston, 1883 . 1.50
The Professor at Breakfast Table (revised). 12mo, Boston,
    1883 .... 1.50
Poems (new ed. Ills). 8vo, Boston, 1885 .... 3.00
Emerson, R. W. Portr. 12mo, Boston, 1885 .... 2.00

Hopkins, F.
Science: a Poem. 4to, Philadelphia, 1762................ 7.50
The Miscellaneous Essays. 3 vols. 8vo, Philadelphia, 1792 .. 5.00

Howe, Mrs. J. W.
Passion Flowers. 18mo, Boston, 1854..................... 1.50
Words for the Hour. 16mo, Boston, 1857................. 1.00
Leonore. 8vo, New York, 1857 .... 1.00

*Howells, William D.
Born at Martinsville, Ohio, 1837.
Poems of Two Friends (with J. J. Piatt). 16mo, Col., 1860.. 10.00
Life of Lincoln and Hamlin. 8vo, 1860 .... 3.50

Venetian Life. 12mo, New York, 1866 .... 2.50
Italian Journey. 12mo, New York, 1867 .... 4.00
No Love Lost. Front. 12mo, New York, 1869 .... 1.50
Suburban Sketches. 12mo, New York, 1871 .... 1.75
Their Wedding Journey. 12mo, Boston, 1872 .... 1.50
Poems. 18mo, Boston, 1873 .... 1.00
Chance Acquaintance. 18mo, Boston, 1873 .... 1.50
A Foregone Conclusion. 12mo, Boston, 1875 .... 1.75
A Day's Pleasure. 16mo, Boston, 1876 .... 1.25
Life of Hayes and Wheeler. Portraits. 16mo, New York,
    1876 .... 1.25
Parlor Car. 18mo, Boston, 1876.......................... 3.00
Out of the Question. 18mo, Boston, 1877................ 1.50
Counterfeit Presentment. 18mo, Boston, 1877........... 1.50
Autobiography (edited). 8 vols. Boston, 1877-8 .... 8.00
Lady of Aroostock. 12mo, Boston, 1879 .... 2.50
Undiscovered Country. 12mo, Boston, 1880 .... 1.50
Fearful Responsibility. 12mo, Boston, 1881 .... 1.50
Chance Acquaintance. 12mo, Boston, 1882 .... 1.50
Dr. Breen's Practice. 12mo, Boston, 1882 .... 1.50
Modern Instance. 12mo, Boston, 1882 .... 1.25
Sleeping Car. 18mo, Boston, 1883 .... 1.50
Woman's Reason. 12mo, Boston, 1883 .... 1.25
Little Girl among Old Masters. Ills. 12mo, Boston, 1884 .. 1.75
The Register. 18mo, Boston, 1884....................... 1.00
Three Villages. 4to, Boston, 1884 .... 1.00
The Elevator. 18mo, Boston, 1885...... ....

Hoyt, R.
Echoes of Memory. 12mo, New York, 1859............... 1.25

Humphreys, David.
Miscellaneous Works. 8vo, New York, 1790 .... 3.50
    "   with additions. 8vo, New York, 1804 .... 3.00

Huntley, Stanley [Spoopendyke].
Spoopendyke. New York, 1881 .... 1.00

Hutton, Lawrence.
Plays and Players. 12mo, New York, 1875 .... 1.50
American Actors' Series [edited]. 6 vols. 12mo, Boston,
    1881-2 .... 6.00
Literary Landmarks of London. 12mo, Boston, 1885........ 1.50

Hyneman, Mrs. R.
The Leper, and other Poems. 12mo, Philadelphia, 1853...... 1.00

Ingersol, Ch. J.
Edwy and Elgiva. 8vo, Philadelphia, 1801............... 3.00
Second War between the United States and Great Britain. 4
    vols. 8vo, Philadelphia, 1845-52 .... 10.00

Poems 1873 75c quo a
Chance a 1.00 quo a Sold at 62c Sotheby's 21 Jn 86

Com Prose 1.00 quo a
Autobiog 75c 1st mul

sketch books - 7 parts - Dg. francis - 9.00

Knickerbocker Loond 1836 Bang 3 Mar 86 2 89
Grayor 35c soiled Vol 3

Ireland, Joseph N.

Records of New York Stage. 2 vols. 8vo, New York, 1866 .. 30.00

*Irving, Washington.
Born at New York 1783, *d.* 1859.

The Literary Picture Gallery etc. to the Visitors of Ballston
    Spa [edited]. 1808 ....
Salmagundi. [with J. K. Paulding], 2 vols. 16mo, New
    York, 1808. .... 12.50
History of New York [Folded Plate]. 2 vols. 16mo, New
    York, 1809 .... 22.50
History of New York [Folded Plate. Revised edition.]. 2
    vols. 16mo, New York 1812 .... 7.50
Sketch Book in 7 Parts. 8vo, New York, 1819............. 15.00
Bracebridge Hall. 2 vols. 8vo, New York, 1822 .... 6.00
Letters of J. Oldstyle. 8vo, New York, 1824 .... 4.50
Tales of a Traveller. 2 vols. 8vo, Philadelphia, 1824 ...... 7.50
Life and Voyages of Columbus. Map. 3 vols. 8vo, New York,
    1828 .... 7.50
Life of Columbus, abridged. 12mo, 1829................. 1.50
A Chronicle of the Conquest of Granada. 2 vols. 12mo, Phil-
    adelphia, 1829 .... 6.50
Voyages and Discoveries of the Companions of Columbus.
    8vo, Philadelphia, 1831 .... 2.50
Alhambra. 2 vols. 8vo, Philadelphia, 1832 .... 5.00
Crayon Miscellanies. 3 vols. 12mo, Philadelphia, 1835...... 4.00
Astoria. 2 vols. 8vo, Philadelphia, 1836 .... 4.00
Captain Bonneville. Map. 2 vols. 12mo, Philadelphia, 1837 . 5.00
Memoirs of Davidson. 1841.......................... 1.50
Legend of Rip Van Winkle, with Darley plates. Folio, New
    York, 1848 .... 3.00
Book of the Hudson (edited). 16mo, New York, 1849 ...... 1.25
    "   (Plate, edited differently). 16mo, New
    York, 1849 .... 1.50
Legend of Sleepy Hollow, with Darley plates. Folio, New
    York, 1849 .... 3.00
Oliver Goldsmith. 12mo, New York, 1849 .... 3.00
Tales of a Traveller (revised ed.) 12mo, New York, 1849 .. 1.25
Mahomet and his Successors. 2 vols. 1850 .... 3.00
Wolfert's Roost. 1855 .... 1.50
Life of Washington. 5 vols. 1855-9...................... 7.50
Life and Letters, edited by P. W. Irving. 4 vols. 12mo, New
    York, 1862 .... 6.00
Spanish Papers. 2 vols. 12mo, New York, 1866 .... 5.00

James, Henry Jr.
Born in New York, 1843.

A Passionate Pilgrim. 12mo, Boston, 1875 .... 1.50
Roderick Hudson. 12mo, Boston, 1876.................... 1.75
The American. 12mo, Boston, 1877 .... 1.50

Watch and Ward.   18mo, Boston, 1878 .... 1.00
The Europeans.   12mo, Boston, 1879 .... 1.25
Confidence.   12mo, Boston, 1880 .... 1.25
Washington Square.   16mo, New York, 1881 .... 1.00
The Portrait of a Lady.   12mo, Boston, 1882 .... 1.50

Jefferson, Thomas.
Born at Shadwell, Va., 1743, *d.* 1826.

Notes on the State of Virginia.   8vo, Philadelphia, 1788...... 3.50
Memoirs, Correspondence, etc. edited by Randolph.   4 vols.
       8vo, Charlot., 1829 .... 5.00
Writings—Autobiography, Correspondence, Messages, etc.
       Edited by H. Washington.   9 vols. 8vo, New York,
       1853-4 .... 16.00

Joseph.
New York Aristocracy.   Ills.   12mo, New York, 1851 ...... 2.00

Judah, S. B.
The Mountain Torrent.   18mo, New York, 1820............. 1.25
The Rose of Arragon.   18mo, New York, 1822 .... 1.50
Gotham and Gothamites.   16mo, New Yrok, 1823 .... 1.50
A Tale of Lexington.   18mo, New York, 1823 .... 1.25

Judd, Sylvester.
Born at Westhampton, Mass., 1813, *d.* 1853.

Margaret: a Tale.   8vo, Boston, 1845..................... 5.00
Philo: an Evangeliad.   12mo, Boston, 1850... .... 1.50
Margaret (revised and enlarged).   2 vols. 12mo, Boston, 1851 . 2.50

Kane, E. K.
Grinel Expedition.   Ills.   8vo, New York, 1854 .... 2.00 – *1.00*
Arctic Exploration.   Ills.   2 vols. 8vo, Philadelphia, 1856 .. 3.50 – *3.50*

Kennedy, J. P.
Born in Maryland, 1795.

Swallow Barn.   1832   .... 2.25
Horse Shoe Robinson.   1835 .... 3.00
Rob of the Bowl.   1838 .... 2.00
Annals of Quodlibet.   1840 .... 1.25

Keese, J.
The Poets of America (edited).   Ills.   12mo, New York, 1840 3.50
       "   2d series.   12mo, New York, 1842.... 4.00

Kettell, S.
Specimens of American Poetry (edited).   3 vols. 8vo, Boston,
       1829 .... 7.50

sketch ??

Knickt?

Gayor?

Rose and 1st new

Key, Fr. S.
Born in Maryland 1779, d. 1843.
Poems. 12mo, New York, 1857 .... 3.00

Knapp, S. L.
The Genius of Masonry. 12mo, Providence, 1828 .... 2.00
Lectures on American Literature. 8vo, New York, 1829 .... 1.50
Tales of the Garden of Kosciuszko. 12mo, New York, 1834 . 1.00

Lamb, Mrs. Martha J.
History of the City of New York. 2 vols. 4to, New York, 1877 15.00

Landon, Melville D. [Eli Perkins.]
Born at Eaton, New York, 1840.
Saratoga 1901. Ills. 8vo, New York, 1872............... 1.75
Eli Perkins at Large. Ills. 12mo, New York, 1875 .... 1.25

Lanza, Mrs. Clara.
Mr. Perkins' Daughter. 12mo, New York, 1881... ... ... 1.00
A Righteous Apostate. 12mo, New York, 1883 .... 1.00

*Lathrop, Geo. P.
Rose and Roof Tree. 12mo, Boston, 1875 .... 2.00
Afterglow. 12mo, Boston, 1876 .... 1.25
A Study of Hawthorne. 12mo, Boston, 1876 .... 1.25
Somebody Else. 12mo, Boston, 1878.................... 1.25
An Echo of Passion. 12mo, Boston, 1882................. 1.25
In the Distance. 12mo, Boston, 1882... .... 1.00
Spanish Vistas. 8vo, New York, 1883 .... 2.00
History of the Union League in Philadelphia. 8vo, Philadel-
   phia, 1883........... .... 1.00
Newport. 12mo, New York, 1884 .... 1.25
True. 12mo, New York, 1884............................ 1.00

Lawson, J.
Giordano. 8vo, New York, 1832......................... 1.25

Lee, Ch.
The Trial of Virtue. 12mo, Hartford, 1806 .... 1.50

Leland, C. G.
The Poetry and Mystery of Dreams. 12mo, Philadelphia, 1856 1.50

Leon, de T. C.
South Songs (edited). 12mo, New York, 1866............. 1.75

Locke, David R. [Petroleum Nasby.]
Born at New York 1833.
Divers Views, etc. Cincinnati, 1865...................... 1.25
Swinging Round the Circle. Boston, 1867................. 1.25
Ekkoes from Kentucky. 12mo, Boston, 1868 .... 1.50

Morals of Abou-Ben-Adhem. 12mo, Boston, 1875 .... 1.25
Nasby in Exile. 8vo, Toledo, 1882....................... 3.00

*Longfellow, Henry W.

Born at Portland, Maine, 1807, d. 1882.

Misc. Poems: selected from The Un. States Literary Gazette,
   with 14 Poems of Longfellow. 16mo, Boston, 1826.... 15.00
Elements of French Grammar (transl.) 12mo, Port., 1830.... 12.50
French Exercises by an Instructor. 12mo, Port., 1830 ...... 15.00
Manuel de Proverbes Dram. 12mo, Port., 1830 .... 12.50
El Serrano de las Alpujarras. 12mo, Brunswick, 1830 ...... 12.50
Cours de Langue Francaise. vol 1. (Wakefield). 12mo, Bost.,
   1832 .... 10.00
   " Proverbes Dram. vol. 2. (2d ed. with add.). 12mo, Bost.,
   1832 .... 5.00
Syllabus de la Gram. Italienne. 12mo, Boston, 1832........ 10.00
Saggi de Novellieri Italiani. 12mo, Boston, 1832 .... 10.00
Coplas de Don J. Manrique (transl.) 16mo, Boston, 1833 .... 10.00
Outre Mer. 2 Nos. 8vo, Boston, 1833 4 .... 35.00
   " 2 vols. 12mo, New York, 1835 .... 9.00
The Voices of the Night. 12mo, Cambridge, 1839 .... 12.50
Hyperion. 2 vols. 12mo, New York, 1839 .... 10.00
Elements of French Grammar (revised ed.) 1840 .... 2.50
Poems on Slavery. 12mo, Cambridge, 1842................. 15.00
Ballads and other Poems. 12mo, Cambridge, 1842.......... 15.00
The Spanish Student. 12mo, Cambridge, 1843 .... 15.00
The Poets and Poetry of Europe (edited). 8vo Phil., 1845 .. 6.00
The Waif (edited). 12mo, Cambridge, 1845 .... 10.00
Poems. Portr. Ills. 8vo, Philadelphia, 1845 .... 10.00
Hyperion (revised ed.) 12mo, Boston, 1845............... 1.25
Poems (new ed.) 8vo, New York, 1846... .... 2.50
The Belfry of Bruges. 12mo, Cambridge, 1846 .... 9.00
Outre Mer (revised ed.) 12mo, Boston, 1846 .... 1.50
Evangeline. 12mo, Boston, 1847........................ 25.00
The Estray (edited). 12mo, Boston, 1847 .... 7.50
Kavanagh. 12mo, Boston, 1849 .... 1.50
The Seaside and Fireside. 12mo, Boston, 1850 .... 1.50
Poems (collected ed.). 2 vols. 18mo, Boston, 1850 .... 2.00
The Golden Legend. 12mo, Boston, 1851................. 5.00
The Song of Hiawatha. 12mo, Boston, 1855 .... 3.50
Prose Work (1st collected). 2 vols. 18mo, Boston, 1857 ... 2.00
The Courtship of Miles Standish. 12mo, Boston, 1858 ..... 2.50
Tales of a Wayside Inn. 12mo, Boston, 1863 .... 1.25
Household Poems. Ills. 16mo, Boston, 1865 .... 1.50
The Divine Comedy of Dante (transl.) 3 vols. 8vo, Boston,
   1867 .... 15.00
Flower de Luce. Ills. 16mo, Boston, 1867................ 1.50
The New England Tragedies. 12mo, Boston, 1868.......... 1.50
Building of the Ship. Ills. (1st sep. ed.) 16mo, Boston, 1870 2.00
The Divine Tragedy. 12mo, Boston, 1871 .... 2.50

Kavanagh soiled 25c
S of H 2.00
S of W I 75c
H. P. 90c
Flower de Louce 75c
N E S 75c
D S 125

Masque 1.00

In the Hole 80c

T for C Rainy 25 Jan 5? (...) 12 4 $0.60
(...) 2.0c 6c

Christus (collected with add.). 3 vols. 12mo, Boston, 1872 ... 3.50
Three Books of Songs. 12mo, Boston, 1872................ 1.00
Aftermath. 12mo, Boston, 1873 .... 3.00
>The Masque of Pandora. 12mo, Boston, 1875 .... 2.00
The Hanging of the Crane. Ills. 12mo, Boston, 1875 ..... 1.25
Poems of Places (edited). 31 vols. 12mo, Boston, 1876-9 .... 25.00
Skeleton in Armor. Ills. (1st sep. ed.) Sm. 4to, Boston, 1877 1.25
Excelsior. (1st sep. ed.) 12mo, Boston, 1878 .... 1.25
Keramos. 12mo, Boston, 1878........................ 1.50
Ultima Thule. 16mo, Boston, 1880 .... 2.00
Poetical Works (subscrip· ed. Ills.) 2 vols. 4to. Bost., 1879-80 15.00
>In the Harbor. 16mo, Boston, 1882 .... 1.00
Prose Works (subscription ed. Ills.) 2 vols. 4to, Boston, 1883 7.50
Michael Angelo. Ills. 4to, Boston, 1884 .... 6,co

Longfellow, S.
Thalatta (with Higginson), 16mo, Boston, 1853 .... 3r00

Lord, W. W.
Poems. 12mo, New York, 1845 .... 1.50
André: a Tragedy. 12mo, New York, 1856........... .... 2.00

Lossing, B. J.
Pictorial Field-Book of Revolution, Ills. 2 vols. 8vo, New
York, 1851-2......................... 12.50
Mount Vernon, etc. Ills. 8vo, New York, 1859 .... 7.50
The Hudson. Ills. 4to, New York, 1866 .... 7.50
Pictorial Field-Book of the War of 1812. Ills. 8vo, New
York, 1868...................................... 7.50
Pictorial Field-Book of Civil War. Ills. 3 vols. 8vo, 1866-8. 12.50
Memorial of A. Anderson, 1st Am. Engraver. Ills. 8vo,
New York, 1872 .... 7.50

Low, S.
Poems. 2 vols. 12mo, New York, 1800.................. 3.50

*Lowell, James Russell.
Born at Cambridge, Mass., 1819.
Class. Poem. Cambridge, 1838 .... 15.00
My First Client. 1840 .... 12.50
A Year's Life. 12mo, Boston. 1841 .... 10.00
Pioneers (edited). 3 Nos. 1843 .... 7.50
Poems. 12mo, Cambridge, 1844 .... 8.50
Conversation on Old Poets. 16mo, Cambridge, 1845 .... 6.00
Bigelow Papers. 12mo, Cambridge, 1848................. 9.00
The Vision of Sir Launfal. 12mo, Boston, 1848 .... 9.00
Poems. 2d series. 12mo, Boston, 1848.................... 7.50
Fable for Critics. 12mo, New York, 1848............... 5.00
    "   with a Preface. 12mo, New York, 1848 ..... 2.00
Poems (1st collected ed.) 2 vols. 12mo, Boston, 1849........ 3.00
The Nooning. 1851 ....

Bigelow Papers. 2d series. 12mo, Boston, 1867 .... 5.00
Under the Willow, etc. 12mo, Boston, 1869 .... 3.00
The Cathedral. 16mo, Boston, 1870 .... 1.50
Among my Books. 12mo, Boston, 1870 .... 4.00
My Study Window. 12mo, Boston, 1871 .... 3.50
Among my Books. 2d series. 12mo, Boston, 1876 .... 2.50
Three Memorial Poems. 16mo, Boston, 1877 .... 1.25
Under the Old Elm, etc. Containing a new poem on Agassiz.
   16mo, Boston, 1885 ....

Lowell, Mrs. Maria.
Poems. Privately printed. 12mo, Cambridge, 1855 .... 3.50

Lowell, R. T. S.
Fresh Hearts that Failed, etc. 12mo, Boston, 1860 .... 1.25

Lunt, G.
Poems. 12mo, New York, 1839 .... 1.50

McCarty, W.
Songs, Odes and other Poems, on National Subjects, collected
   from various sources. 3 vols. 16mo, Philadelphia, 1842 5.00

Mackenzie, Alexander Slidell.
Born at New York 1803, d. 1848.

A Year in Spain. 2 vols. 12mo, Boston, 1829... .... 2.00
The American in Spain. 2 vols. 12mo, New York, 1835 .... 1.25
The American in England. 2 vols. 12mo, New York, 1835 .. 2.00 – 1.00
The Life of Comm. Perry. 2 vols. 18mo, New York, 1841 .. 2.00 – .30

Madison, James.
Born at Port Conway, Va., 1751, d. 1836.

Letters and other Writings (collected). 4 vols. 8vo, Philadelphia, 1865 .... 12.50

Markoe, Peter.
The Patriotic Chief. 8vo, Philadelphia, 1783 .... 7.50
Miscellaneous Poems. 8vo, Philadelphia, 1787 .... 10.00
The Times. 8vo, Philadelphia, 1788 .... 7.50

Marsh, G. P.
Born at Woodstock, Vt., 1801, d. 1882.

Lectures on the English Language. 8vo, New York, 1860 .. 2.50
Origin of English Language. 8vo, New York, 1862 .... 2.00
Man and Nature. 8vo, New York, 1864 .... 2.00

Martenze, C.
Cannon Flashes and Penn-dashes. 12mo, New York, 1866 .... 1.00

Mather, Cotton.
Born in Massachusetts 1663, d. 1728.
Psalterium Americanum. 12mo, Boston, 1718 .... 30.00

3 Men Poems 80c

21 Ja 86 '36

F. G. 1.⁰⁰ slightly stained
Ruf G B 2.²⁵ fine cond
Sircando 75c Bind'g loose

Mathew, C.
Poems on Man. 12mo, New York, 1843 .... 1.50

Matthews, Brander,
Theatres of Paris. 16mo, New York, 1880 .... 1.00
French Dramatists. 8vo, New York, 1881 .... 1.50
Poems of Amercan Patriotism. 12mo, New York, 1882 ...... 1.25
In Partnership (with H. Bunner). 1884.................... 1.00

May, Mrs. C.
The American Female Poets (edited). Ports. 8vo, Philadelphia, 1848 .... 2.25

Mead, Ch.
Mississippian Scenery: a Poem. 12mo, Philadelphia, 1819 .. 2.00

Melville, Herman.
Typee. 12mo, New York, 1846 .... 1.50
Omoo. 12mo, New York, 1847 .... 1.50
Israel Potter. 12mo, New York, 1855 .... 1.50
The Piazza Tales. 12mo, New York, 1856 .... 1.50

Miles, Geo. H.
Mohamed: a Tragedy. 12mo, Boston, 1850............... 1.00

Miller, J.
Songs of the Sierras. 12mo, Boston, 1871........ .... 1.50
The First Families of the Sierras. 1.50

*Mitchell, Donald G. [Ik Marvell.]
Born at Norwich, Conn., 1822.
Fresh Gleanings. 8vo, New York, 1847 .... 2.75
Reveries of a Bachelor. Ills. 12mo, New York, 1850 ...... 3.50
Battle Summer. 12mo, New York, 1850 .... 2.50
Dream Life. 12mo, New York, 1851.......... .... 2.50
Fresh Gleanings (with new preface). 12mo, New York, 1851 . 1.75
The Lorgnette. Ills. 2 vols. 12mo, New York, 1851 ...... 5.00
Fudge Doings. Ills. 2 vols. 12mo, New York, 1855 ...... 2.75
My Farm at Edgewood. 12mo, New York, 1863............ 1.50
Seven Stories. 12mo, New York, 1864 .... 1.50
Wet Days at Edgewood. 12mo, New York, 1865 .... 1.75
Dr. Johns. 2 vols. 12mo, New York, 1866 .... 2.50
Rural Studies. 12mo, New York, 1867................... 1.75
About Old Story Tellers. Ills. 12mo, New York, 1877 ...... 1.25
Bound Together. 12mo, New York, 1884.................. 1.50

Moore, Frank.
Songs of American Revolution (ed.) 12mo, New York, 1856 . 1.75
Lyrics of Loyalty (ed.) 18mo, New York, 1864 .... 1.50
Rebel Rhymes and Rapsodies (ed.) 18mo, New York, 1864.. 2.00
Personal and Political Ballads (ed.) 18mo, New York, 1864.. 1.50
Songs of the Soldiers (ed.) 18mo, New York, 1864......... 1.50

Moore, George H.
Notes on the History of Slavery in Massachusetts. 8vo, New
   York, 1866 ....   3.00

Moos, H. M.
Mortara, with Choice Poems. 12mo, Cincinnati, 1860 ......   1.25

Morris, G. P.
Born in Pennsylvania 1802, d. 1864.
The Deserted Bride. 8vo, New York, 1838 ....   1.50
Little Frenchman and His Water Lots. Ills. 12mo, Philadel-
   phia, 1839 ....   1.50
American Melodies (a Selection). 18mo, New York, 1841 ....   1.25
The Songs and Ballads. 8vo, New York, 1844 ....   1.25

Morton, S. G.
Crania Americana. (Map and 78 plates.) Folio, Philadelphia,
   1839 .... 40.00

*Motley, John Lathrop.
Born at Dorchester, Mass., 1814, d. 1877.
Morton's Hope. 2 vols. 12mo, New York, 1839 ....   7.50
Merry Mount. 2 vols. 12mo, Boston, 1849 ....   6.50
The Rise of the Dutch Republic. 3 vols. 8vo, New York, 1856 12.50
Causes of the Civil War. 8vo, New York, 1861 ....   2.50
History of United Netherland. 4 vols. 8vo, New York, 1861-8 12.50
Historic Progress and Am. Democracy. 8vo, New York, 1869   1.50
The Life of John Barneveldt. 2 vols. 8vo, New York, 1874 ..   9.00

Mowatt, Mrs. A. C.
Armand. 12mo, New York, 1851 ....   1.00
Plays (enlarged ed.) 18mo, Boston, 1855 ....   1.25

Munfree, Mary N. [Ch. E. Craddock.]
Stories in the Tennessee Mountains. 12mo, Boston, 1884 ....   1.25

Nack, J.
The Legend of the Rocks. 12mo. New York, 1827..........   1.50
Earl of Rupert. 12mo, New York, 1839 ....   1.25

Nason, E.
A Monogram on Our National Songs. 8vo, Albany, 1869 ....   1.00

Neal, Joseph C.
Charcoal Sketches. Ills. 12mo, Philadelphia, 1838 ....   1.50
Petter Ploddy, and other Oddities. 12mo, 1844 ....   1.50

Newell, [Orpheus C. Kerr.]
Orpheus Kerr Papers. 12mo, New York, 1862 ....   1.00
Avery Glibun. 12mo, 1867 ....   1.00
Smoked Glass. 12mo, New York, 1868 ....   1.25
The Cloven Foot. 12mo, New York, 1870...................   1.00

Noah, M. M.

The Fortress of Sorrento. 18mo, New York, 1808............ .... 2.00
The Grecian Captive. 18mo. New York, 1822 .... 1.50

Nordhoff, Ch.

The Communistic Societies of the United States. 8vo, New
York, 1875 .... 3.00

Norton, C. E.

Dante's Vita Nuova (transl.) 8vo, Boston, 1867.... .... 3.50

Norton, Ch. L.

Canoeing in Kanuckia (with Habberton). 12mo, New York.
1878.. 1.25

Noyes, J. H.

History of American Socialism. 8vo, Philadelphia, 1870...... 2.50

Nye, Bill.

B. Nye and His Mule Boomerang. 8vo, Chicago, 1881 ...... 1.50

O'Calaghan. E. B.

History of New Netherland. Ills. 2 vols. 8vo, New York,
1846-8 .... 5.00
A List of Editions of Holy Scripture. Printed in America to
1860. 8vo, Albany, 1861 .... 7.50

Osborn, L.

The Confessions of a Poet. 12mo, Philadelphia, 1835 .... 3.50
The Vision of Rubeta. 8vo, Boston, 1838.................... 5.00
Arthur Carryl. 12mo, New York, 1841 .... 2.50
The Silver Head. 12mo, New York, 1867... .... 1.25

Osgood. Mrs. F. S.

The Poetry of Flowers. 12mo, New York, 1841 .... 1.25
The Snow Drop. 16mo, Providence, 1842 .... 1.00
Poems. 16mo, New York, 1850 .... 1.00

Paine, R.T.
Born at Taunton, Mass., 1773, d. 1811.

The Invention of Letters. 4to, Boston, 1795 .... 7.50
A Monody. 8vo, Boston, 1811 .... 2.00

Palfrey, John G.
Born in Massachusetts 1766, d. 1881.

History of New England. 4 vols. 8vo, Boston, 1859-76 ...... 12.50

*Parkman, Francis.
Born in Boston, Mass., 1823.

The California and Oregon Trail. 12mo, New York, 1849 .... 2.50
Hist. of the Conspiracy of Pontiac. 8vo, Boston, 1864........ 2.50

Vassal Norton.   8vo, Boston, 1856............................   2.50
Pioneers of France in the New World.   8vo, Boston, 1865   ....   2.50
Book of Roses.   12mo, 1866 ....   1.50
The Jesuits in North America in 17th Century.   8vo, 1867   ....   2.50
Historic Account of Bouquet's Expedition.   8vo,   Cinncinnati,
    1868..   2.50
Discovery of the Great West.   8vo, Boston, 1869 ....   4.00
Montcalm and Wolfe.   2 vols. 8vo, Boston, 1885 ....   4.00

Parris, S. B.

Miscellaneous Poems and Essays.   12mo, Plymouth, 1829 ....   1.50

Paulding, James K.
Born at Pleasant Valley, N. Y., 1778, *d.* 1860.

Salmagundi (with Irving).   2 vols. 16mo, New York, 1808....   12.50
The Lay of the Scottish Fiddle.   18mo, Philadelphia, 1813....   3.50
Jokeby.   18mo, Boston, 1813...............................   3.50
History of John Bull and Brother Jonathan.   18mo, New York,
    1813.... ....   5.00
United States and England.   8vo, New York, 1815 ... .   2.50
Letters from the South.   2 vols. 12mo, New York, 1817 ......   2.00
The Blackwoodsman.   12mo, Philadelphia, 1818 ....   1.75
Salmagundi. 2d series.   12mo, New York, 1819 ....   2.75
New Mirror for Travellers.   12mo, New York, 1828 ....   2.00
Tales of the Good Woman.   12mo, New York, 1829..........   2 00
The Dutchman's Fireside.   12mo, New York, 1831 ....   5.00
American Comedies (with W. L. Paulding).   8vo, Philadelphia,
    1847...   2.50

Payne, J. H.
Born at New York, 1791, *d.* 1852.

Lovers' Vows.   18mo, Baltimore, 1809 ....   2.50
Accusation.   18mo, Boston, 1818......................   2.00
Adeline.   18mo, New York, 1822 ....   1.75
Clari (with Home, Sweet Home).   18mo, New York, 1823....   5.00
Ali Pacha.   18mo, New York, 1823.........................   1.25
Richelieu.   18mo, New York, 1826 ....   1.25

*Percival, J. G.
Born in Connecticut 1795, *d.* 1856.

Poems.   18mo, New Haven, 1821............. ....   3.50
Clio. No. 1.   12mo, Charleston, 1822.....................   2.75
Clio. No. 2.   12mo, New Haven, 1822 ....   2.75
Poems.   8vo, New York, 1823 ....   5.00
Clio. No. 3.   12mo, New York, 1827.....................   2.00
The Dream of a Day, etc.   12mo, New Haven, 1843 ....   2.00
Poetical Works (collected).   2 vols. 18mo, Boston, 1859......   1.50

Phelps, Ch. H.

Californian Verses.   12mo, S. Francisco, 1882 ....   1.25

Loether f— 8 2vols in 1 ½ cf 1.00
" " " 8— 2 vols @ .75 ha rf C (Banyo)
Tales 1.00   Jos ? Banyo .57
Puritan and his daughter N Y 1849 2 vols in 1. 75c
Westward He - 2 vols -16°- 1.50

↗ Soii F.. ...==

Haji: Ali Kissan $1.55 per vol

Phillips, Wendel.
Speeches, Lectures and Letters. Portr. 12mo, Boston, 1863..   2.00

Pierce, W. L.
The Year: a Poem. 12mo, New York, 1813 ....   2.50

Pierpont, J.
The Anti slavery Poems. 16mo, Boston, 1843 ....   1.50

*Pike, A,
Prose Sketches and Poems. 12mo, Boston, 1834 ....   4.50
Nugae. 12mo, Philadelphia, 1854.........................   3.00
The Life Wake. 8vo, Washington, 1859 ....   3.00

*Poe, Edgar A.
Born at Boston 1809, d. 1849.
Tamerlane, and other Poems. 16mo, Boston, 1827 ....
Al Aaraaf, Tamerlane, and Minor Poems. 16mo, Balt. 1829.
Poems (called 2d ed.) 16mo, New York, 1831 ....   25.00
Southern Literary Messenger (edited). Richmond, 1836 ....   7.50
New York Quarterly Review (edited). 1837...............   5.00
The Narrative of A. G. Pym. 12mo, New York, 1838 ......   17.50
The Conchologist. 1st Book. Plates. 16mo, Philadelphia,
     1839 ....   12.50
Gentleman's Magazine (edited). Philadelphia, 1839-40 ......   7.50
Tales Grotesque and Arabesque. 2 vols. 12mo, Philadelphia,
     1840 ....   35.00
Graham Magazine (edited). Philadelphia, 1841-42 . ...   5.00
Tales. 12mo, New York, 1845 ....   7.50
Raven, and other Poems. 12mo, New York, 1845 ... .   12.50
Broadway Magazine (edited). New York, 1845 ....   5.00
Eureka. 12mo, New York, 1848 ....   7.50
Works (collected), with introduction of Lowell, Willis, etc.,
     2 vols. 12mo, New York, 1850.....................   5.00
The Literati. 12mo, New York, 1850...................   5.00
Gordon Pym, and Miscellanies (collected). 12mo, New York,
     1856 ....   3.00
Works (new and complete ed. with introd. by R. H. Stoddard).
     6 vols. 12mo, New York, 1885 ....   9.00

Pollard, E.
Black Diamonds. 12mo, New York, 1859 ....   1.00
Southern Hist. of the War. Ills. 4 vols. 8vo, New York, 1863-6   12.50
Lost Cause. Ills. 8vo, New York, 1867 ....   2.50

*Prescott, W. H.
Born at Salem, Mass., 1796, d. 1859.
History of the Reign of Ferdinand and Isabella. 3 vols. 8vo,
     Boston, 1837 ....   15.00
History of the Conquest of Mexico. 3 vols. 8vo, New York,
     1843 ....   10.00

Critical and Miscellaneous Essays. 8vo, New York, 1845 .... 3.00
History of the Conquest of Peru. 2 vols. 8vo, New York, 1847 7.50
History of the Reign of Philip II. 3 vols. 8vo, Boston, 1855-8 9.00
The Life of Charles V. (Supplement to Robertson). 3 vols.
    8vo, Boston, 1857.................................. 5.00

Prime, W. C.

The Owl Creek Letters. 12mo, New York, 1848............ 4.00
Coins, Medals and Seals, Ancient and Modern. Ills. 4to, New
    York, 1861.. 5.00

Putnam, Mrs. M. L.

The Bond Maid. 16mo, Boston, 1844...................... 1.25

Quincy, J. P.

Lyteria. 12mo, Boston, 1854 .... 1.00

*Randolph, A. D. F.

Hopefully Waiting. 16mo, New York, 1867 .... 1.25

Read, T. B.

Poems. 16mo, Boston, 1847............................... 2.50
Lays and Ballads. 12mo, Philadelphia, 1849 .... 2.00
The Wagoner of the Alleghanies. 16mo, Philadelphia, 1862.. 1.00
Summer Storm, Sheridan's Ride, etc. 12mo, Philad. 1865.... 1.50

Rice, G. E.

Myrtilla. 12mo, Boston, 1854 .... 1.25
Mount Vernon. 12mo, Cleveland, 1858................ ... 1.25

Richards, G.

The Declaration of Independence. 8vo, Boston, 1793........ 4.00

Richards, W. C.

Electron. 12mo, New York, 1858 .... 1.00

Ricord, Mrs. E.

Zamba: a Dramatic Poem. 12mo, Boston, 1842 .... 1.00

Robinson, S.

Hot Corn. Life in New York. 12mo, New York, 1854........ 1.25

Rogers, G.

G. Washington Crowned. Portr. 12mo, New York, 1849.... 1.00

Sabine, L.

American Loyalists. 8vo, Boston, 1847 .... 3.50

Sanderson, John.

Biography of the Signers of the Declaration of Independence.
    Portraits. 9 vols. 8vo, Philadelphia, 1820-27......... 20.00

Hnf C of P Krisson @ 1.<u>60</u> per unit

Read JB Sylvia Phil 1857 75c
'Summer Storm' 1.<u>00</u>

Saunders Kissam 20c

Masq 75c

Sands, R. C.

The Bridal of Vaumond. 18mo, New York, 1817 .... 2.00

Sargent, E.

Velasco: a Tragedy. 8vo, New York, 1839 .... 1.50
The Light of the Light-House. 8vo, New York, 1844 ...... 1.25

Saunders, F.

Salad for the Social. Ills. 12mo, New York, 1856.......... 1.50

Savage, James.

Genealogical Dictionary of the First Settlers of New England.
    4 vols. 8vo, Boston, 1860 .... 30.00

Saxe, J. G.

Poems. 16mo, Boston, 1850.............................. 1.50
The Money King. 16mo, Boston, 1860 .... 1.00
The Flying Dutchman. 12mo, New York, 1862 .... 1.50
The Masquerade, and other Poems. 12mo, Boston, 1866 ..... 1.25

Schoolcraft, H. R.

The Rise of the West. 12mo, New York, 1841.............. 2.00
Alhalla. 12mo, New York, 1843....................... 1.50
Historical and Statistical Information Respecting the History,
Condition and Prospects of Indian Tribes of the United States.
    Ills. 6 vols. 4to, Philadelphia, 1851-7 .... 60.00

Scott, Genio C.

Fishing in American Waters. Ills. 8vo, New York, 1869 .. 3.00

Scoville, Joseph. [W. Barrett.]

Old Merchants of New York City. 5 vols. 12mo, New York,
    1863-6... 12.50
Vigor: a Novel. 12mo, New York, 1864 .... 4.00

Seward, W. H.
Born at Florida, N. Y., 1801, d. 1872.

Works. 3 vols. 8vo, New York, 1853 .... 6.00

Shaw, H. W. [Josh Billings.]

Josh Billings, His Sayings. 1866... .... 1.50
Josh Billings on Ice. 12mo, New York, 1870 .... 1.25

*Sigourney, Mrs. L. H.
Born at Norwich, Conn., 1791, d. 1865.

Moral Pieces, in Prose and Verse. 12mo, Hartford, 1815 .... 2.50
Biography of A. M. Hyde. 18mo, 1816.................... 1.25
The Square Table. 12mo, 1819 .... 1.25
Traits of Aborigenes. 12mo, Cambridge, 1822.............. 1.25
Sketch of Connecticut. 12mo, 1824 .... 1.50
Poems. 12mo, Boston, 1827.............................. 1.25

Biography of Females. 12mo, 1829........................   1.25
Biography of Pious Persons. 2 vols. 12mo, 1832 ....   1.00
Letters to Young Ladies. 12mo, 1833...............   1.00
Evening Reading in History. 1833......   1.00
How to be Happy. 1833 ....,...........   1.25
Memoir of Phebe Hammond. 1833 ......   1.00
Sketches and Tales. 12mo, Philadelphia, 1834..............   2 00
Select Poems. 12mo, Philadelphia, 1834 ....   1.50
Poetry for Children. 16mo, 1834.......   1.00
Tales and Essays for Children. 16mo, 1834 ....   1.00
History of M. A. Antoninus. 1835 ....   1.25
Olive Buds. 1836........................   1.25
Zinzendorph. and other Poems. 16mo, 1836 ....   1.25
Letters to Mothers. 1838 ....   1.25
Girls' Reading Book. 18mo, 1838 ....   1.00
Boys' Reading Book. 1839 ....   1.00
Pocahontas, and other Poems. 12mo, New York. 1841 ......   1.25
Pleasant Memories of Pleasant Lands. 12mo, 1842 ....   1.25
Poems. 1842.....................   1.25
Child's Book. 1844 ....   1.00
Scenes in My Native Land. 12mo, Boston, 1845 ....   1.25
Voice of Flowers. 32mo, 1845................   1.25
The Lovely Sisters. 32mo, 1845 ....   1.25
Voices of Home on the Sea. 12mo, Boston, 1845 ....   1.50
Myrtis, etc. 12mo, 1846 ....   1.00
Weeping Willow. 32mo, 1846... ....   1.25
Water-Drops. 12mo, 1847 ....   1.25
Poems. Ills. by Darley. (Collected.) 8vo, Philadelphia, 1849   4.00
Whisper to a Bride. 18mo, 1849 ....   1.50
Letters to My Pupils. 16mo, 1850 ....   1.00
Poems for the Sea. Ills. 12mo, Hartford, 1850 .....,.....   1.25
Examples of Life and Death. 12mo, 1851..................   1.00
Olive Leaves. 16mo, 1851 ....   1.00
Memoir of Mrs. H. N. Cooke. 12mo, 1852 ....   1.25
Voices of Home. 12mo, Hartford, 1852..................   1.25
The Faded Hope. 16mo, 1852............. ....   1.00
The Western Home, and other Poems. 12mo, Phila. 1852 ..   1.50
Past Meridian. 1854 ....   1.00
Sayings of the Little Ones. 1854........................   1.00
Examples from 18th and 19th Centuries, 1857..............   1.00
The Daily Councellor. 1858 ....   1.25
Gleanings. 1860...,.................   1.25
The Man of Uz, and other Poems. 12mo, Hartford, 1862....   1.50
Selections from Various Sources. 1863 ....   1.25
Letters of Life. 1866 ....   1.25

*Simms, W. G.
Born at Charleston, S. C., 1806, d. 1870.

Lyrical and other Poems. 18mo, Charleston, 1827 ....   3.50
Early Lays. 12mo, Charleston, 1827 ....   2.50

The Yen 65c gerund
Meli 65c " "

The Vision of Cortez. 12mo, Charleston, 1829.............. 2.00
The Tricolor. 1830 .... 2.00
Slavery in the South. 1831 .... 2.00
Atalantis. 12mo, New York, 1832 .... 2.50
Michael Bonham. 2.00
Martin Faber. 12mo, New York, 1833 .... 2.00
Poems. 12mo, Charleston, 1833 .... 3.50
Guy River. 2 vols. 12mo, New York, 1834............. 2.25
The Partisan. 2 vols. 12mo, New York, 1835..... ...... 2.25
The Yemassee. 2 vols. 12mo, New York, 1835 .... 2.00
Melichampe. 2 vols. 12mo, 1836 .... 2.50
Richard Hurdis. 2 vols. 12mo, Philadelphia, 1838 .... 2.00
Carl Werner. 2 vols. 12mo, 1838 .... 2.00
Damsel of Darien. 2 vols. 12mo, Philadelphia, 1839..... .. 2.50
Pelayo. 2 vols. 12mo, New York, 1839 .... 2.00
Southern Passages and Pictures. 12mo, New York, 1839 ... 2.00
History of South Carolina. 12mo, Charleston, 1840 ...... 1.50
Castle Dismal. 12mo, 1840 .... 1.50
Border Beagles. 2 vols. 12mo, 1840 .... 1.75
The Kinsmen. 2 vols. 12mo, Philadelphia, 1841.......... 2.25
Confession. 2 vols. 12mo, 1841 .... 2.00
The Social Principle (oration). 1842 .... 1.25
Beauchampe. 2 vols. 12mo, 1842 .... 2.00
Geography of South Carolina. 12mo, Charleston, 1843 ...... 1.75
Donna Florida. 18mo, Charleston, 1843 .... 1.75
The Swords of American Independence (oration). 1844.. .. 1.50
Life of F. Marion. 12mo, New York, 1844 .... 1.00
Views and Reviews. 1st series. 12mo, New York, 1845 .... 1.25
The Wigwam and Cabin. 1st series. 12mo, Charleston, 1845 1.50
Southward-Ho! 12mo, New York, 1845 .... 1.25
Count Julian. 2 vols. 1845 .... 2.00
Helen Halsey. 12mo, 1845 .... 1.50
Grouped Thoughts and Scattered Fancies. 18mo, Richm. 1845 1.25
Areytos. 18mo, Charleston, 1845 .... 2.00
Views and Reviews. 2d series. 12mo, 1846 .... 1.25
Life of J. Smith. 12mo, New York, 1846 .... 1.00
The Wigwam and Cabin. 2d series. 12mo, 1846 .... 1.25
Self Development (oration). 1847 .... 1.25
Life of Chevalier Bayard. 12mo, New York, 1847 .... 1.25
The Battle of Fort Moultrie (discourse). 1.50
Supplement to the Plays of Shakspeare (edited). 8vo, New
York, 1848 .... 1.75
Lays of the Palmetto. 12mo, 1848 .... 1.50
The Eye and the Wing. 8vo, New York, 1848 ... . 1.50
The Cassique of Accabee. 8vo, New York, 1848............ 1.25
Life of N. Greene. 12mo, 1849 .... 1.25
Father Abbott. 1849 .... 1.25
Sabbath Lyrics. 12mo, Charleston, 1849 .... 1.50
Charleston and Her Satyrists. 1849 .... 2.00
The Lily and the Totem. 12mo, New York, 1850 .... 1.25

The City of the Silent. 8vo, Charleston, 1850 ....   1.50
Katherine Walton. 12mo, 1851 ....   1.25
Norman Maurice. 8vo, Richmond, 1851 ....   1.00
The Golden Christmas. 12mo, Charleston. 1852 ....   1.00
As Good as a Comedy. 12mo, Philadelphia, 1852 ....   1.25
Egeria. 12mo. Philadelphia, 1853 ....   1.50
Vasconselos. 12mo, 1853 ....   1.50
The Book of My Lady. 12mo, Philadelphia, 1853 ....   1.25
Marie de Berniere. 12mo, 1853 ....   1.25
Poems, etc. 2 vols. 12mo, New York, 1853.................   2.50
South Carolina in the Revolution. 8vo, 1854 ....   2.00
The Sword and the Distaff. 12mo, Charleston, 1854 ....   1.25
The Forayers. 12mo, 1855 ....   1.25
Eutaw. 12mo, 1856 ....   1.25
Charlemont. 12mo, 1856 ....   1.50
History of South Carolina (with additions). 12mo, New York,
   1859 ....   1.25
The Cassique of Kiawah. 12mo, 1859 ....   1.25
Poems. 12mo. Charleston, 1860 ....   1.50
The Ghost of My Husband. 16mo, New York, 1866 ....   1.00
War Poetry of the South (edited). 12mo, New York, 1867 ..   1.50

Smith, Joseph, Jr.
Born at Sharon, Vt., 1805, d. 1844.

The Book of Mormon. 12mo, Palmyra, 1830.............. 25.00

Smith, Mrs. E. O.

Poetical Writings. 18mo, New York, 1845 ....   1.25

Smith, Seba. [Major J. Downing.]

Life and Letters of J. Downing. 12mo, Boston, 1833........   1.75
Powhattan. 12mo, Boston, 1841 .... 1.50
Away Down East. 12mo, 1843 ....   1.50
My 30 Years Out of the Senate. 12mo, New York, 1859 ....   1.25
Major J. Downing of the Downingsville Militia. 1864........   1.25

Sparks, Jared.
Born at Willington, Conn., 1789, d. 1866.

An Account of the Manuscript Papers of G. Washington, left at
   Mount Vernon. 8vo, Boston, 1827 ....   3.00
The Diplomatic Correspondence of the American Revolution
   (edited). 12 vols. 8vo, Boston, 1829-30.............. 17.50
The Life of Gouverneur Morris. Portr. 3 vols. 8vo, Boston,
   1832 ....   4.00
The Library of American Biography (edited. Out of 60 Lives—8,
   namely: Allen, Arnold, Marquette, De La Salle, Pulaski,
   Ribault, Lee and Ledyard—written by himself·) 1st se-
   ries. 10 vols. 16mo, Boston, 1834-7 .... 10.00
   Do.   Do.   2d series. 15 vols. 16mo, Boston, 1844-8 15.00
Correspondence of American Revolution (edited). 4 vols. 8vo,
   Boston, 1853 ....   7.50

Spofford, Mrs. H. E.

Thief in the Night. 16mo, Boston, 1872 .... 1.00
Amber Gods. 16mo, New York, 1881 .... 1.00

Sprague, Charles.

Curiosity. 8vo, Boston, 1829 ... . 2.50
An Ode. 8vo, Boston, 1830 .... 1.25
Poetical and Prose Writing. (collected and revised). 12mo,
    Boston, 1850... .... 1.25

Squire, E. G.
Born at Bethlehem, N. Y., 1821.

Ancient Monuments of the Mississippi Valley (with E. H. Da-
    vis). 48 plates. 4to, Washington, 1848 .... 25.00
Aboriginal Monuments of the State of New York. 14 plates.
    4to, Washington, 1849 .... 5.00
The Serpent Symbol, etc., in America. Ills. 8vo, New York,
    1851 .... 5.00
Nicaragua: its Monuments, etc. Ills. 2 vols. 8vo, New York,
    1852 .... 4.50
Notes on Central America. Ills. 8vo, New York, 1855...... 4.00
Waikna. Ills. 12mo, New York, 1855............... 1.50
The States of Central America. Ills. 8vo, New York, 1858 . 7.50
Honduras— Descriptive, Historical, etc. Map. 12mo, New
    York, 1870.. 2.50
Peru: Land of Incas. Ills. 8vo, New York, 1876 .... 4.00

*Stedman, Edmund C.
Born in Connecticut 1833. .

Poems: Lyrical and Idyllic. 12mo, New York, 1860........ 2.50
The Prince's Ball. Ills. 12mo, New York, 1860 .... 1.50
The Battle of Bull Run. 12mo, New York, 1861........ 3.50
Alice of Monmouth. 12mo, New York, 1864 .... 2.00
Reconstruction Letter (priv. printed). 8vo, New York, 1866 . 3.50
The Blameless Prince, etc. 12mo, Boston, 1869 .... 2.00
Rip Van Winkle. (Colored Plates). 4to, Boston, 1870 ...... 3.50
Poems. 16mo, Boston, 1873............................. 1.50
Cameos. 16mo, Boston, 1874 .... 2.00
Victorian Poets. 12mo, Boston, 1876.................... 1.50
O. B. Frothingham, 16mo, 1876........................ 1.25
Mrs. Browning. 32mo, Boston, 1877 .... 1.00
Favorite Poems. 32mo, Boston, 1877.................. .... 1.00
Hawthorne, and other Poems. 12mo, Boston, 1877 .... 1.00
E. A. Poe. 16mo, Boston, 1881 .... 1.00
Poems (household ed.) Ills. 1884 .... 1.25
Poems (priv. printed). 8vo, New York, 1885 .... 7.50

Stephens, Alexander.

War between the States. Ills. 2 vols. 8vo, Philadelphia,
    1868-70 .... 3.50

*Stephens, J. L.

Born in New Jersey, 1805, d. 1852.

Incidents of Travels in Egypt, Arabia, etc. 2 vols. 12mo, New
York, 1837 .... 1.50
" in Greece, Turkey, Russia, etc. 2 vols.
12mo, New York, 1838 .... 1.50
" in Central America, etc. 2 vols. 8vo, New
York, 1841 .... 6.00
" in Yucatan. 2 vols. 8vo, New York, 1843 5.00

Stiles, H. R.

Letters from the Prison Ships of the Revolution (edited). 2 vols.
4to, New York, 1865 .... 10.00 - *4.00*
History of the City of Brooklyn. Ills. 3 vols. 8vo, Brooklyn,
1867 .... 7.50
Bundling—its Origin, etc., in America. 12mo, Albany, 1869.. 5.00

Stillman, W. J.

Poetical Localities of Cambridge (edited). 4to, Boston, 1875.. 3.00

*Stockton, Frank R.

Ting-a-ling. 16mo, Boston, 1870 .... 2 00
Round-about Rambles. 4to, New York, 1872 ... . 1.50
What Might Have Been Expected. 16mo, New York, 1874 .. 1.25
Tales Out of School. 4to, New York, 1875 .... 1.50
Rudder Grange. 16mo, New York, 1879 .... 1.25
A Jolly Fellowship. 12mo, New York, 1880 .... 1.25
The Lady or the Tiger. 16mo, New York, 1884............ 1.00
The Story of Viteau. 12mo, New York, 1884 .... 1.00

*Stoddard, R. H.

Foot-Prints. 8vo, New York, 1849.............. .... 2.50
Poems. 16mo, Boston, 1852............................. 1.50
Songs of Summer. 16mo, Boston, 1857 .... 1.50
The King's Bell. 12mo, New York, 1863 .... 1.50
The Story of Little Red-Riding-Hood. Ills. 4to, New York,
1864 .... 2.50
Abraham Lincoln. 4to, New York, 1865 .... 1.50
The Children in the Wood. Ills. 4to, New York, 1866...... 1.50
Putnam the Brave. Ills. 4to, Boston, 1870............... 1.25
The Book of the East, etc. Boston, 1871 .... 1.50
Poems (collected ed.) 8vo, New York, 1880................. 3.00

Story, I.

An Eulogy. 8vo, Salem, 1800............................. 2.00

Story, J.

A Parnassian Shop. 12mo, Boston, 1801 .... 1.50

Story. W. W.

Nature and Art. 8vo, Boston, 1844....................... 1.50
Poems. 12mo, Boston, 1847............... .... 1.75

Poems 75c
Mrs R H S' Sms Men NY '65 $1.00

Relig Poems 75c

Frontenac. Bougie

*Stowe, Mrs. H. E. B. [Chr. Crowfield.]
Born at Litchfield, Conn., 1812.

Mayflower. 12mo, New York, 1849	1.75
Uncle Tom's Cabin. 2 vols. 12mo, Boston, 1852.............	5.00
A Key to the Uncle Tom's Cabin. 1853................... .	1.00
Peep into Uncle Tom's Cabin. 16mo, Boston, 1853..........	1.00
Sunny Memories of Foreign Lands. 2 vols. 12mo, Bost. 1854.	2.00
The Christian Slave. 12mo, Boston, 1855	1.25
Dred. 2 vols. 12mo, Boston, 1856	2.00
Our Charley and What to do with Him. 12mo, Boston, 1858 .	1.25
The Minister's Wooing. 12mo, Boston, 1859	1.25
The Pearl of Orr Island. 12mo, Boston, 1862	1.00
Agnes of Sorrento. 12mo, Boston, 1862...................	1.00
Reply on behalf of Women in America. 1863	1.25
The Ravages of a Carpet. 1864	1.25
House and Home Papers. 16mo, Boston, 1864.............	1.00
Religious Poems. 16mo, Boston, 1865	1.25
Little Foxes. Ills. 16mo, Boston, 1865	1.25
Queer Little People. 4to, Boston, 1867...................	1.25
Daisy's First Winter. 12mo, 1867	1.00
The Chimney Corner. 12mo, Boston, 1868	1.00
Men of Our Times. 8vo, Hartford, 1868	1.50
Old Town Folks. 12mo, Boston, 1869	1 00
The American Women's Home. 12mo, Philadelphia, 1869 ..	1.25
Lady Byron Windicated. 12mo, Boston, 1869..............	1.00
Pink and White Tyranny. 12mo, Boston, 1871	1.00
My Wife and I. 1871....................................	1.00
Palmetto Leaves. 12mo, Boston, 1873....................	1.00
We and Our Neighbours. 12mo, New York, 1875............	1.00
Poganuc People. 12mo, New York, 1878..................	1.00

*Street, Alfred B.
Born at Poughkeepsie, N. Y., 1811.

The Burning of Schenectady. 12mo, Albany, 1842..........	2.50
Drawings and Tintings. 8vo, New York, 1844	2.00
Poems. 8vo, New York, 1845.............	2.50
Frontenac. 12mo, New York, 1849	2.50
Poems (collected ed.) 2 vols. 16mo, New York, 1867	2.50

Sumner, Charles.
Born in Massachusetts 1811, d. 1874.

Orations and Speeches. 2 vols. 12mo, Boston, 1850	2.00
White Slavery in Barbary States. 12mo, Boston, 1853	1.50
Prophetic Voices Concerning America. 12mo, Boston, 1874 ..	1.50
Complete Works. Portr. 15 vols. 8vo, Boston, 1870-83	40.00

Sweet, Alexander E.

Sketches from Texas Siftings (with A. Knox). 12mo, New
York, 1882... 1.00

Tappan, W. B.

New England. 18mo, Philadelphia, 1819....	3.00
Songs of Judah. 18mo, Philadelphia, 1820	2.00
Poems. 12mo, Philadelphia, 1822	2.50
Lyrics. 12mo, Philadelphia, 1822	2.25
Poetry of the Heart. 12mo, Worcester, 1845...........	1.25
Poetry of Life. 16mo, Boston, 1848	1.25

*Taylor, Bayard.
Born in Pennsylvania 1825, d. 1878.

Ximena. 12mo, Philadelphia, 1844........................	4.00
View a Foot. 1846.....................................	1.50
Ballads. 1848	3.50
Rhymes of Travel. 12mo, New York, 1849	2.50
The American Legend. 12mo, Cambridge, 1850............	2.50
Eldorado. 1850	1.50
Romances, Lyrics and Songs. 16mo, Boston, 1852..........	2.50
Poems. 1852	3.00
Journey to Central Africa. 12mo, New York, 1854..........	2.00
Land of the Saracens. 12mo, New York, 1855............	1.25
Poems of the Orient. 12mo, Boston, 1855............	1.50
India, China and Japan. 1855	1.75 – .75
Poems of Home and Travel. 12mo, Boston, 1855	2.50
Northern Travels. 1858................................	1.50
Greece and Russia. 1859	1.50
Home and Abroad. 1860	1.25
" 2d series. 1862......................	1.00
The Poets' Journal. 12mo, Boston, 1863	1.50
Hannah Thurston. 1863	1.00
John Godfrey's Fortunes. 12mo, New York, 1865	1.50
The Story of Kennett. 12mo, New York, 1866	1.50
Picture of St. John. 12mo, Boston, 1866	1.00
Colorado. 1867	1.25
Frithiof's Saga (edited). 12mo, New York, 1867............	1.50
By-Ways of Europe. 1869..............................	1.50
Joseph and His Friend. 12mo, New York, 1870	1.25
The Ballad of A. Lincoln. 4to, Boston, 1870	1.25
Faust of Goethe (transl.) 2 vols. 8vo, Boston, 1871	5.00
Beauty and the Beast. 12mo, New York, 1872	1.00
Travels in Arabia. 1872	1.25
The Masque of the Gods. 12mo, Boston, 1872.............	1.00
Lars and Pastorals of Norway. 12mo, Boston, 1873	1.50
South Africa. 1873.................................	1.25
The Prophet. 1874..................	1.25
Egypt and Iceland. 1874	1.25
Home Pastorals. 12mo, Boston, 1875.....................	1.50
Echo Club. 1876.....................................	1.00
Stories for American Boys. 1876	1.00
The National Ode. 4to, Boston, 1877.................	1.50
Boys of Other Countries. 1877............................	1.00

Poems of H & J 1 $\underline{25}$

Colorado 75 c.

Prince Deukalion. 1878.................................. 1.00
Picturesque Europe (edited). 3 vols. 4to, New York, 1880 .. 35.00
Critical Essays and Literary Notes. 1880 .... 1.25
Who Was She? 1884 .... 1.00
Melodies of Verse. 1884...................... .... 1.00

Thomas, Isaiah.
The History of Printing in America. 2 vols. 8vo, Worcester,
    1810 .... 10.00

Thompson, M. H. [Q. K. Philander Doesticks.]
Doesticks—What He Says. 12mo, New York, 1855 .. .. 1.25
The Elephant Club. 12mo, Philadelphia, 1856.............. 1.00
Plu-Ri-Bus-Tah. 12mo, New York, 1856.................. 2.00
Nothing to Say. 12mo, New York, 1857................... 1.25
Witches of New York. 12mo, New York, 1859............ 1.00

*Thoreau, Henry D.
Born in Massachusetts 1817, *d.* 1862.
Week on Concord and Merrimac Rivers. 12mo, 1849........ 6.00
Walden. 12mo, Boston, 1854.............................. 4.25
Excursions. 1863.. 3.50
Maine Woods. 1864...................................... 3.00
Cape Cod. 12mo, Boston, 1865........................... 3.00
Letters to Various Persons. 12mo, Boston, 1865............. 2.75
Yankee in Canada. 12mo, Boston, 1866................... 2.75
Early Spring in Massachusetts. 12mo, Boston, 1881. .... 1.75
Summer. 1884... 1.25

Ticknor, George
Born in Massachusetts 1791, *d.* 1871.
History of the Spanish Literature. 3 vols. 8vo, Boston, 1849 9.00
Life of W. H. Prescott. 4to, Boston, 1864.. .... 5.00

Tourgee, A. W.
Born in Ohio, 1838.
Fools Errand. 12mo, New York, 1879.................... 1.25
Bricks without Straw. 12mo, New York, 1880.............. 1.25
Hot Plowshares. 12mo, New York, 1883....... .... 1.25
Appeal to Cæsar. 12mo, New York, 1884 .... 1.00

Townsend, G. A. [Gath.]
Tales of the Chesapeake. 12mo, New York, 1880............ 1.00
Bohemian Days. 16mo, 1881.............................. 1.00
President Cromwell. 8vo, New York, 1885................. 3.00

Trowbridge, J. T. [Paul Creyton.]
Neighbor Jackwood. 12mo, Boston, 1857..... .... 1.50
The Vagabonds. 4to, New York, 1864..................... 1.25
The Story of Columbus. 4to, Boston, 1870................. 1.00
Emigrants Story, and other Poems. 12mo, Boston, 1881..... 1.00

Trumbull, John
Born at Woodbury, Conn., 1750, d. 1831.

An Elegy on the Times. 8vo, New Haven, 1775 .... 5.60
McFingal. 12mo, Hartford, 1782 .... 5.00

Trumbull, John.
Born at Lebanon, Conn. 1756, d. 1843.

Autobiography, Reminiscences and Letters. Plates. 8vo,
   New York, 1841 .... 4.00

*Tuckerman, Bayard.

History of English Prose Fiction. 12mo, New York, 1882. ... 1.50

*Tuckerman, Henry Theodore,
Born at Boston 1813, d. 1871.

The Italian Sketch-Book. 12mo, Philadelphia, 1835 .... 4.00
Isabel, or Sicily. 12mo, Philadelphia, 1839 .... 3.50
Rambles and Reveries. 12mo, 1841 .... 3.50
Thought on the Poets. 16mo, New York, 1846 .... 3.00
Artist Life : Sketches of American Painters. 12mo, New York,
   1847 .... 3.00
Italian Sketch-Book [with additions]. 12mo, New York, 1848 2.00
Characteristic of Literature. 16mo, Philadelphia, 1849 ...... 3.00
The Optimist. 12mo, New York, 1850 .... 2.50
The Life of Silas Talbot. 12mo, 1850 .... 3.00
Characteristic of Literature. 2d series. 12mo, 1851 .... 3.50
Poems. 12mo, Boston, 1851 .... 1.50
A Memorial of H. Greenough. 12mo, New York, 1853 ...... 1.50
Mental Portraits. 12mo, 1853 .... 2.00
Leaves from a Dairy of a Dreamer. 1853 .... 3.00
A Month in England. 12mo, New York, 1853 .... 2.25
Essays, Biographical, Critical. 8vo, Boston, 1857 .... 2.50
The Character and Portraits of Washington. 4to, New York,
   1859 .... 7.50
The Rebellion : its Latent Causes, Etc. 12mo, New York, 1861 1.25
America and her Commentators. 8vo, New York, 1864 ...... 2.50
Dr. Francis' Old New York, with Memoirs by H. T. Tuckerman
   12mo, New York, 1865 .... 3.00
The Criterion. 12mo, New York, 1866 .... 1.50
Maga Papers about Paris. 12mo, New York, 1867 .... 3.00
Book of the Artist : American Artist Life. 8vo, New York,
   1867 .... 4.00
Life of J. P. Kennedy. 12mo, New York, 1871 .... 1.50

Tyler, Moses C.

A History of American Literature, 1607 to 1765. 2 vols. 8vo,
   New York, 1879 .... 5.00

Upham, T. C.

American Sketches. 18mo, New York, 1819 .... 2.00

Warner C D In the Wilderness Boston 1878
new 75c

Very, J.
Essays and Poems. 16mo, Boston, 1839.. .... 3.00

Wallace, W. R.
The Battle of Tippecanoe. 12mo, Cincinnati, 1815.......... 2.00
Meditations. 12mo, New York, 1851...................... 1.50

Ware, H.
Poem at the Celebration of Peace. 8vo, Camb. 1815......... 2.00
The Vision of Liberty. 8vo, Boston, 1824.................. 2.00

Warner, Ch. D.
Born in Massachusetts 1829.
My Summer in a Garden. 16mo, Boston, 1870.............. 3.00
Back-Log Studies. 4to, Boston, 1872..................... 2.00
Mummies and Moslems. 8vo, Hartford, 1876 .... 2.50
Washington Irving. Portr. 16mo, Boston, 1882 .... 1.25

Warner, Miss Susan. [Wetherell.]
Born at New York 1818, d. 1885.
The Wide, Wide World. 1850...................... .... 3.50

Warren, Mrs. Mercy.
The Adulateur. 8vo, Boston, 1773 .... 5.00
Poems: Dramatic and Miscell. 16mo, Boston, 1790 .... 3.50
History of the American Revolution. 3 vols. 8vo, Bost. 1805. 5.00

Washington, George.
Born in Virginia 1732, d. 1799.
The Journal of Major G. W. sent by R. Dinwiddie to the Commandant of Ohio, etc. 8vo, Williamsburg, Va., 1754..
A Circular Letter Addressed to the Governors of the Several States on His Retiring from Public Business. 8vo, Philadelphia, 1783................................. 25.00
Official Letters to American Congress. 2 vols. 12mo, Boston, 1795 .... 5.00
Epistles Domestic, Confidential and Official. 8vo, New York, 1796 .... 5.00
Farewell Address—Address to the People of the United States. 8vo, Philadelphia, 1796 ...... 5.00
The Will of G. W., with a Schedule of His Property. 12mo, Alex. 1800.................................. 3.00
Fac-simile of Washington's Accounts. Folio, (Washingt. 1833) 4.00
The Writings of G. W., edited by Sparks. 12 vols. 8vo, Bost. 1837 .... 17.50
Diary of Washington 1789-90 (priv. pr.) 8vo, N. Y., 1858 .. 15.00

Webb, C. H.
The Wickedest Women in New York. Ills. 12mo, New York, 1868 .... 1.00

Webster, Daniel.
Born at Salisbury, N. H., 1782, d. 1852.

Webster, Noah.
Born at Hartford, Conn., 1758, d. 1843.

Weekes, R.

Welby, Mrs. A. B.

Wetmore, P. M.

Wheatley, Mrs. Phillis.
Born 1754, d. 1784.

White, Horace.

White, R. G.

* Whitman, Mrs. S.

Webster Daniel several pamphlets speeches 25¢ ea

* Whitman, Walt.
Born at West Hills, L. I., N. Y., 1819.

Leaves of Grass—12 Poems. Portr. Folio, Brooklyn, 1855 . .	15.00
" 32 Poems. Portr. 16mo, New York, 1856 ..	10.00
" 154 Poems. Portr. 12mo, Boston, 1860	3.50
Drum-Taps, Lincoln Hymn, etc. 12mo, Washington, 1865 ..	3.50
When Lilacs, etc. 12mo, Washington, 1865-6	4.00
Leaves of Grass—235 Poems. 12mo, New York, 1867	4.00
After all not to Create Only. 12mo, Boston, 1871	1.00
Leaves of Grass—263 Poems. 12mo, Washington, 1871	10.00
Democratic Vistas. 8vo, Washington, 1871	5.00
Passages to India, etc. 12mo, Washington, 1872......	6.00
As a Strong Bird on Pinions Free, etc. 12mo, Washingt. 1872	3.00
Memoranda During the War. 8vo, Washington, 1875	3.00
Leaves of Grass—288 Poems and Two Rivoulets. Portr. 2 vols.	
12mo, Camden, 1876	10.00
" 293 Poems. 12mo, Boston, 1881-2	3.50

* Whittier, John G.
Born at Haverhill, N. H., 1807.

Legends of New England. 12mo, Hartford, 1831............	20.00
Literary Remains of J. G. Brainard. 12mo, Hartford, 1832 ..	7.50
Moll Pitcher. 32mo, 1832................................	25.00
Justice and Expediency. Haverhill. 1833	5.00
Mogg Megone. 32mo, Boston, 1836	12.50
Poems. Front. 12mo, Boston, 1837	10.00
View of Slavery and Emancipation (edited). New York, 1837.	3.00
Letters from J. Q. Adams (edited). Boston, 1837............	3.00
Address at the Opening of Penn Hall. 1838	3.50
Poems. 12mo, Philadelphia, 1838	9.00
North Star. the Poetry of Freedom (edited). 16mo, Philadel-	
phia, 1840.......................................	2.50
Moll Pitcher and the Minstrel Girl (revised ed.) 16mo, Phila-	
delphia, 1840	5.00
The Voices of Freedom. Philadelphia, 1841	3.00
Lays of My Home, etc. 12mo, Boston, 1843	7.50
The Stranger in Lowell. 12mo, Boston, 1845	7.50
The Supernaturalism of New England. Sm. 4to, New York,	
1847	7.50
Leaves from Margarett Smith Journal. 12mo, Boston, 1849 ..	5.00
Poems Illustrated. 8vo, Boston, 1849	7.50
Old Portraits and Modern Sketches. 12mo, Boston, 1850....	3.50
Songs of Labor. 12mo, Boston, 1850....................	6.00
Memoir of R. Dillingham, with Introductory Poem by Whittier.	
12mo, Philadelphia, 1852	2.00
Little Eva: Uncle Tom's Guardian Angel, with Music. Folio,	
Boston, 1852	5.00
The Chapel of the Hermits. 12mo, Boston, 1853............	2.00
Literary Recreations, etc. 12mo, Boston, 1854	3.50
A Sabbath Scene. 12mo, Boston, 1854	3.50

The Panorama. 12mo, Boston, 1856 .... 2.00
Poetical Works (collected ed.) 2 vols. 16mo, 1857 .... 2.50
Home Ballads, etc. 12mo, Boston, 1860 .... 4.50
Sound now the Trumpet (for Fremont Campaign). 186? 3.00
In War Time. 12mo, Boston, 1864 .... 1.50
National Lyrics. 16mo, Boston, 1865 .... 2.50
Prose Works (collected). 2 vols. 16mo, Boston, 1866....... 2.50
Snow Bound. 12mo, Boston, 1866 .... 1.25
Maud Muller. 8vo, Boston, 1867 .... 1.25
The Tent on the Beach. 12mo, Boston, 1867 .... 1.25
Among the Hills. 12mo, Boston, 1869 .... 1.25
Ballad of New England (1st sep. ed.) 12mo, Boston, 1870 .. 1.50
Miriam, and other Poems. 12mo, Boston, 1871 .... 1.25
Child Life—Poems (edited). Boston, 1871 .... 3.50
The Journal of Jno. Woolman (edited). 12mo, Boston, 1871.. 2.56
The Pennsylvania Pilgrim. 12mo, Boston, 1872 .... 2.00
Child Life—Prose (edited). 1873..................... 2.00
Agassiz Memorial (with T. W. Parsons). 16mo, Cambridge,
     1874 .... 5.00
Hazel Blossoms. 12mo, Boston, 1875 .... 1.50
Songs of Three Centuries (edited). 8vo, Boston, 1876 ...... 2.50
Mabel Martin (1st sep. ed.) 12mo, Boston, 1876............ 1.25
Centennial Hymn. 1876 .... 1.50
Indian Civilization (with Introduction by Whittier). 1877.... 2.50
The Vision of Erchard. 12mo, Boston, 1878................ 1.50
The King's Missive. 12mo, Boston, 1881 .... 1.00
Bay of Seven Islands. 12mo, 1883..................... 1.25
Letters of L. M. Child (edited). 1883................... ... 1.25
Jack in the Pulpit (edited). 1884..................... 1.00

*Willis, Nathaniel P.

Born at Portland, Maine, 1806, d. 1867.

Sketches. 8vo, Boston, 1827........................... 7.50
The Legendary (edited). 2 vols. 12mo, Boston, 1828........ 3.50
Fugitive Poetry. 8vo, Boston, 1829 .... 5.00
Poem delivered before Brown University, etc. 8vo, New York,
     1831 .... 5.00
Pencillings by the Way. 2 vols. 12mo, Philadelphia, 1836 .. 3.00
Inkling of Adventure. 2 vols. 12mo, New York. 1836 ...... 2.25
Melanie, and other Poems. 12mo, New York, 1837 .... 1.50
Torteza. 18mo, New York, 1839 .... 1.75
Bianca Visconti. 12mo, New York, 1839 .... 1.25
A L'Abri or Tent Pitched, 12mo, New York, 1839 .... 1.50
Romance of Travel. 12mo, New York, 1840 .... 1.50
Poems of Passion. 12mo, New York, 1843 .... 1.50
The Sacred Poems. 8vo, New York, 1843............... 1.00
Lady Jane, and other Poems. 8vo, New York, 1844 .... 1.25
Lecture on Fashion. 8vo, New York. 1844 .... 1.00
Dashes of Life. 12mo, New York, 1845................. 1.25
Rural Letters. 12mo, New York, 1849 .... 2.00

Tenton B 75c
Annong H 75c

Mabel Martin 2nd Autograph Copy
Vuf E 100
Kingo M 75c

Winter W The Queen's Domain and other Poems
NY 1859 75c
" Geo Arnold, Poems edited by NY 1866
2vol 75c ea

Edwin Boothroft 100

People I Have Met. 12mo, New York. 1850................ 2.00
Life Here and There. 12mo. New York, 1850.............. 2.00
Hurry-graphs. 12mo, New York, 1851 .... 1.25
Trenton Falls. 12mo, New York, 1851 .... 1.00
Memoranda of the Life of J. Lind. 12mo, Philadelphia, 1851 . 1.25
A Summer Cruise in the Mediterraneum. 12mo, New York,
    1853 .... 1.25
A Health Trip to the Tropics. 12mo, New York, 1853...... 1.75
Fun Jottings. 12mo, New York, 1853 .... 1.25
Famous Persons and Places. 12mo, New York. 1854 .... 1.25
Out Doors at Idlewood. 12mo, New York, 1854 .... 1.00
Ephemera. 12mo, New York. 1854 .... 1.00
The Rag-Bag. 12mo, New York, 1855 .... 1.25
Paul Fane. 12mo, New York, 1856.................... 1.25
The Convalescent. 12mo, New York, 1859 .... 1.00
The Poems (collected ed.) 8vo, New York, 1868............ 2.50

Winslow, B. D.
Class Poem. 8vo, Cambridge, 1835 .... 2.00

Winter, W.
Poems. 12mo, Boston, 1855....... .... 2.00
E. Booth in 12 Dramatic Characters. Ills. 4to, Boston, 1872 3.50
Trip to England. 12mo, Philadelphia, 1879.............. 1.00
E. Irving. Portr. 16mo, New York, 1885 .... 1.25

Winthrop, J.
A Journal of the Transactions and Occurances in New England
    Colonies 1630-40. 8vo, Hartford, 1790 .... 8.00
The History of New England 1630-40, with Notes by J. Savage.
    2 vols. 8vo, Boston, 1825-6 .... 7.50

*Winthrop, Theodore.
Born at New Haven, Conn., 1828, d. 1861.

Cecile Dreeme. 16mo, Boston, 1861 .... 3.50
John Brent. 16mo, Boston, 1862...................... 2.00
Edwin Brothertoft. 16mo, Boston, 1862 ... . 1.75
The Canoe and the Saddle. 12mo, Boston, 1862........... 1.75
Life in the Open Air, etc. Portr. 12mo, Boston, 1863 ...... 1.50

Wolcott, Elisa and Sarah.
The Two Sisters' Poems. 18mo, New Haven, 1830 .... 5.00

Woodhull, Victoria C.
Origin, Tendencies and Principles of Government. 8vo, New
    York, 1871 .... 1.00

Woolsey, Theodore D.
Born at New York 1801.

Political Science. 2 vols. 8vo, New York, 1878.............. 3.50
Communism and Socialism. 12mo, New York, 1881 .... 1.00

*Woodsworth, S.
Born 1785, *d.* 1842.

Beasts and Law. 12mo, New York, 1811.................... 2.50
Quarter Day. 8vo, New York, 1812 .... 1.50
Bubble and Squeak. 12mo, New York, 1814 .... 1.50
The Complete Coiffeur. 12mo, New York, 1817 .... 1.50
The Poems. 12mo, New York, 1818 .... 2.00

Yellot, G.
The Paradise of Fools. 12mo, Boston, 1841............... 2.00
The Professor of Insanity. 12mo, Baltimore, 1856 .... 2.25

Young, A.
Chronicles of the Pilgrim Fathers 1602-25. 8vo, Boston, 1841. 5.00
  "   of the First Planters of Massachusetts Bay, 1602-36.
    8vo, Boston, 1846................................. 5.00

Bibliographical and Biographical Works not necessarily 1st Editions, but relating to American Literature and Men of Letters.

Adams, O. F. Brief Hand-book of American Authors.
12mo, Boston, 1884 .... .75

Allibone, S. A. Critical Dictionary of English Literature
(British and American Authors). 3 vols. 8vo, Philadelphia, 1871 .... 20.00

American First Editions. Longfellow Collectors' Hand-
book, Compiled and Published by **W. E. Benjamin.**
12mo, New York, 1885 .... 1.50

American First Editions.—A Catalogue of First Editions
of above 300 American Authors, Compiled and Published by **Leon and Brother.** 12mo, New York, 1885   1.00 – 1.00

Beers, H A. Nathaniel P. Willis. 16mo, Boston...... 1.25

Bigelow, J. William C. Bryant (in prep.) 16mo, Boston   1.25

Brinley, G. Catalogue of American Library. 3 vols. 8vo,
priced, Hartford, 1881 .... 10.00

Bucke, R. M. Walt. Whitman. 12mo, Philad. 1883 ..   1.75

Burton, W. E. Cyclopedia of Wit and Humor of America, etc. 8vo, New York......................... 5.00

Cable, G. W. William G. Simms. 16mo, Boston...... 1.25

Clemens. Famous Funny Fellows of America. 12mo,
Cleve., 1882 .... 1.25

Duyckinck, E. Cyclopedia of Am. Literature. 2 vols.
8vo, 1866 .... 10.00

Drake, F. S. Dictionary of American Biography, with Supplement. 8vo, Boston, 1872 .... 5.00

Elliot, C. W. American Interiors—Views of Libraries of Longfellow, Bryant, Mitchell, etc., with an Essay on the Library, etc. 4to, Boston.......................... 10.00

Green, A. G. Catalogue of Library—Contains the First Prominent Collection of American Poetry. Priced, 8vo, New York, 1869 .... 4.00

Harris, C. Fiske. Index to American Poetry and Plays. 12mo, Providence, 1874............................ 5.00

Higginson, T. W. Marg. Fuller-Ossoli. 16mo, Bost. 1.25

Holmes, O. W. Ralph W. Emerson. 16mo, Boston .. 1.25

Homes of American Authors. Ills. 4to, New York, 1853 . 5.00
  "   "   Ills. 4to, Hartford, 1855. 3.00

Hudson, F. Journalism in the United States from 1690 to 1872. 8vo, New York 4.00

Hynes, J. Pseudonyms of Authors. 8vo, New York, 1882 2.00

Kelly. American Catalogue of Books, Original and Reprints, Published in the United States from 1861 to 1871. 2 vols. 8vo, New York 10.00

Kennedy, W. S. Henry W. Longfellow. 12mo, Bost. 1.25
  "   "   John G. Whittier. 12mo, Bost. 1883. 1.25
  "   "   Oliver W. Holmes. 12mo, Bost. 1883. 1.25

Leypoldt, F. Publishers' Trade List Annual, 1873-1885. 13 vols. 8vo, New York................ 20.00
  "   "   American Catalogue of Books in Print and for Sale—Authors, Titles and Subjects. 3 vols. 4to, New York, 1876 1885...................... ...... 50.00

Lounsbury, T. R. J. F. Cooper. 16mo, Boston .... 1.25 - *90*

Lowell, J. R. Nathaniel Hawthorne (in prep.) 16mo, Boston 1.25

Poole, W. F. Index to Periodical Literature. 8vo, New York, 1853 .... 4.00
  Do.   Do.   8vo, Boston, 1882 .... 15.00

Public Libraries of United States. 2 vols. 8vo, Wash. 1876. 3.50

Rees, J. The Dramatic Authors of America. 12mo, New York, 1845 .... 1.50

Roorbach. Bibliotheca Americana—Catalogue of American Publications, including Reprints and Original Works—1820-61. 4 vols. 8vo, New York, 1852-61 .... 40.00

Sabin, J. Bibliography of Bibliography. 8vo, New York, 1877 .... 1.50
  "   A Dictionary of Books Relating to America from its Discovery to Present Time. 83 Parts. 8vo, New York, 1869-85, per Part 2.00

ERRATA.

PAGE 11—Line 35, Artemus, etc. : for $30.00 read ——

" 11— " 40, The Embargo, etc. : for $3.00 read $30.00.

" 13— " 13, Principles, etc.: for $2.50 read $7.50.

" 27— " 38, Hopkins, etc.: for Hopkins read Hopkinson.

" 28— • 19, Chance, etc. : the whole line should be omitted.

" 35— " 1, Mathew, etc.: for Mathew read Mathews.

" 37— " 35, Born in, etc.: for 1776 read 1796.

" 37— " 40, History, etc.: for 1864 read 1851.

" 42— " 37, The Western, etc.: for 1852 read 1854.

" 43— " 45, The Cassique, etc.: for 1848 read 1849.

" 51— " 4. The Battle, etc.: for 1815 read 1837.

" 53— " 22. Moll etc. for 32mo, read 8vo.

www.ingramcontent.com/pod-product-compliance
Lightning Source LLC
Chambersburg PA
CBHW020805020726
47495CB00008B/2598